THE TENANTS OF 7C

Alice Degan

CONTENTS

1. The Tenants of 7C   7

2. The Siege of 7C   49

3. Birds of a Feather   111

4. 7C Goes Down   116

5. The Future   213

6. The Present   217

THE TENANTS OF 7C

CLARE CAME TO WORK every day feeling pleased with herself. She would walk through the glass doors wearing one of her carefully chosen, fashionably casual work ensembles, and look around the high-ceilinged, brick-walled interior of Stake Inc., and sigh with satisfaction. Only inwardly, of course; if you wanted to fit in at Stake, Clare had realized early on, you had to behave as if you thought you were really just a little bit too good to be working there. It was an attitude she didn't find hard to cultivate.

On that particular morning, though, she was having trouble. She sat in her car, scrolling through the list of locations on her phone, wondering whether she *was* good enough. You never got very many instructions at Stake, but even for them, this was a little thin. "Use your instincts," Seevers had told her. "Consult the software, but don't rely on it. When in doubt, go with your gut." Which sounded like it might be an ass-covering way of saying that the software wasn't any good. He had sat on the edge of her desk and waxed poetic about getting back to the basics, pounding the pavement, diversifying core offerings.

So she was finally getting a chance to do field agent work. It was what she had been waiting for—but she had expected a little more fanfare when the time finally came for her to do it. Instead what she'd got was a confusing app that had slowed her phone to a glacial speed, and Seevers' vague pep-talk. But it was fine. Maybe he didn't think she was going to even get far enough to need real instructions. Maybe—probably—it was a kind of test. She'd show him he'd been wrong to underestimate her.

The places on her list were all over the city: some were just intersections, others whole neighbourhoods. As she scrolled down again, *Kensington Market* caught her eye. Well, that wasn't too bad. She needed to pick up some spices to make that Indian thing for the potluck on the weekend, and the Sobeys near her apartment didn't carry all of them. She pocketed her phone, decision made, and turned the key in the ignition.

In some moods, Clare liked Kensington Market in a way that she found hard to explain. The grubbiness of it, the weird smells: it seemed out of character for her to like it, but sometimes she did. She found a place on an upper storey of the parking garage, and headed out into the market.

The snow had stopped by the time she came out of the House of Spice with her black cardamom pods and fenugreek. She clamped one glove under her arm and fumbled with her slowed-down phone. It was a weekday morning, and cold, so the market was not very busy. Clare stationed herself unobtrusively outside an army surplus shop and scrolled through the settings to DETECTION—MAP MODE.

After some moments of CONNECTING TO NETWORK and ACQUIRING DATA, she was finally rewarded with a map of the surrounding streets, and a blinking blue triangle that must represent her target. It appeared to be in the middle of a block; but the image was not very detailed, and couldn't be zoomed. (Yep, the software was a piece of crap; Seevers had been right.) Though maybe it was showing her something that was inside of a shop or a house.

She felt a small buzz of excitement as she set off down one of the central streets of the market, heading towards the location of the blinking triangle. This was real fieldwork, after all. Anything could happen. She was in the front lines now. It would have seemed more appropriate if it had been after dark, or at least a grey, overcast day, rather than unexpectedly sunny in spite of the cold. But you had to start somewhere. Outside a fruit and vegetable store she stopped to check her phone again. The blue triangle was still blinking in the middle of the block; whatever it was, it didn't appear to be on the move.

She turned the corner and walked until she had come level with the triangle on what seemed to be the closest street. She was outside of a very tumbledown health-food store, with faded posters in the windows advertising vitamins and herbal weight-loss pills. She looked at it doubtfully. It was the sort of store that looked closed even when it was open. If what was causing the blinking blue triangle was inside there, Clare doubted that it was really what she was looking for after all.

But it wasn't in the health-food store. She walked all the way to the freezers at the back, and when she consulted her phone there, the red dot that represented her was still not quite on top of the blue triangle. Something behind the store, maybe?

There was an alley down one side of the store, partially blocked by a delivery van which Clare had to squeeze apprehensively past. The snow had frozen into dirty ruts down the middle of the pavement, which was little more than a network of potholes.

She arrived at the rear of the store. There was another alley here, with the backs of stores on one side, and on the other a row of small, connected houses, totally hidden from the street. Some of them had been jauntily painted and outfitted with window boxes and lace curtains; others looked neglected and pitiful. Down at the end of the row, the very last house bore a faded sign above its front window. Clare walked down to the end of the alley and looked up at the sign. *Heaven and Earth Bakery*, it said.

Compared to the Heaven and Earth Bakery, the health food store had looked positively welcoming. This place looked more than closed; it looked abandoned. The front window was half covered in newspapers, and there was graffiti on the door. But a smell of fresh baking—magnificent, irresistible fresh baking—curled out from somewhere inside the dingy house. And when Clare looked down at the scanner, the red dot was just touching the edge of the blue triangle. This was what she had been looking for.

The door opened, with a gently tinkling chime, into a small, warm, crowded shop. It was furnished with a haphazard mixture of Ikea chairs and plastic patio tables with garish vinyl tablecloths. The only decoration on the white walls was an out-of-date calendar and a faded piece of weaving. On the whole, rationally, Clare was unimpressed. But the part of her that revelled in the dirty streets of Kensington was jumping for joy. The smell of baking in the air was so good it made the whole place beautiful. Clare threaded her way between the full tables of the front room to the doorway which led into a back room. Here there were a few more tables, not all full, and a glass-fronted counter crammed with the most luscious baked goods she had ever seen. It was hard to explain why they looked so good. There were plain cakes, with no fancy icing or chocolate shavings, crusty loaves of bread, and different kinds of buns. But you could tell, somehow, that it would all taste better than any cake or bread or bun that you had ever had.

The app was now flashing an unhelpful icon like a No Parking sign. Clare pocketed her phone, hung her purse off the back of a chair at an empty table, and went to look at the cakes. A teenaged girl with stringy, unconvincing black hair emerged from a door behind the counter, hefting a tray of buns. She gave Clare a resentful look and clattered the tray down on top of the counter.

"Do you want something?" she asked, with a thick accent that Clare thought of as Russian.

Clare ordered a slice of cake for here, and tried to get a coffee but was told with an incredulous sneer that they only served tea.

"I guess that will have to do, then."

"Sit. I bring it to you."

She sat, and tried to get the app working again while she waited for the unfriendly girl to bring her cake and tea. She called up INTERIOR MODE, THREAT CLASSIFICATION, and SHORT RANGE IDENTIFICATION in succession—not that she had any clue what they did—but all showed the same flashing No Parking icon. Piece of *crap*.

Another woman had come out from the back of the bakery by the time Sulky Girl had finished cutting Clare's cake, and she brought the plate and the mug of tea over herself. She was stopped as she came out from behind the counter by a greasy-haired man in a blue windbreaker, who seemed to have some urgent question to ask her. She arrived at Clare's table finally, smiling and shaking her head.

"He has it fixed in his mind that we used to serve dim sum here," she told Clare as she set down the plate and mug. "'When are you going to bring back the dim sum?' he asks every time he comes in. I try to explain that we're not a Chinese restaurant, but … " She shrugged.

She was a slight woman a little older than Clare, with dark hair cut in a short, careless style. She was dressed in an almost outrageously frumpy combination of a long floral skirt and a bulky grey sweatshirt. Maybe she hadn't heard that you could buy fashionable maternity clothes, Clare though charitably. She wasn't hugely pregnant yet, but she was getting there.

"Can I get you anything else?" the woman asked. "And please don't say *barbecue pork buns*."

"I'm fine, thanks," said Clare. On an impulse she added: "This place is pretty hard to find."

The woman cocked up one dark eyebrow quizzically. "We do try to keep it that way."

"What? Don't you like having customers?"

She studied Clare a moment longer. "How did you find out about my bakery?"

Her bakery? She couldn't be the owner, Clare thought. Dressed like that? But then, the bakery wasn't much to look at, either.

"Oh, I just happened by."

The woman looked for a moment as though she didn't believe her. Then she smiled. "Enjoy your cake."

Clare did enjoy the cake. She had chosen something which she had thought was chocolate, but it turned out to be a sort of gingerbread. It was just as she had imagined from the smell: quite simple, but nearly perfect. The tea she didn't care for; it tasted strangely of flowers.

Her cake finished, she sat thinking about what to do next. According to the map, she was at the right place, but that was worth nothing if she couldn't visually verify and classify the actual target. There might be a glitch in the app; it might have been reading residual energy from something that was here a long time ago. If that was even the right term. Energy? I mean, she thought, it must be something like that. "Go with your gut," Seevers had said. Back to the basics, blah blah. She needed to come back with a lot more information than she had now, if she was going to turn this into the basis for a successful hunt. There was just one other thing she thought she could rely on, which might save her having to creep back to the office, mission unaccomplished, to make her boss's day. There was the smell.

It wasn't something that you sensed in the same way as an ordinary smell; you had to concentrate in a certain way, a bit like listening to the sound of your own heart. Clare had never heard the principle behind it explained, though she assumed it was something that all of Stake's field agents could do. She tried it now. The result was strange; there was definitely something here, but it was hard to tell what. When she focussed her attention, she still smelled the warm, sweet, food scents of the bakery. It was like hearing music when you tried to listen for your heartbeat. As far as she knew, it shouldn't have been possible. She closed her eyes and concentrated harder.

At first she got nothing, then underlying the bakery smell there was something a little salty, faintly like the sea. It was unfamiliar, not what she was looking for, but obviously somehow the same *type* of thing. It grew stronger for a moment, and then, just briefly, she caught a whiff of the earthy, metallic smell that she was used to: the vampire smell. She opened her eyes. The frumpy pregnant woman was standing beside her table, regarding her with faint amusement. Out of the corner of her eye, Clare saw the sulky girl disappearing back into the kitchen. Well, yes, that would be typical. The stringy black hair and everything.

"How did you like your cake?" the frumpy woman asked.

"Oh, um ... " Clare felt her cheeks heating up with embarrassment. "Excellent. It was excellent."

"Can I bring you anything else?"

"No, no—just the bill, please."

The woman took Clare's empty plate and fork. "How would you like to pay?"

Clare glanced at the ancient-looking cash register on the counter. There was no sign of a debit machine, no Mastercard sticker on the register. It seemed a dumb question. "Cash?"

The woman nodded and went away.

The cake proved surprisingly cheap, and it looked to Clare, from the hand-written bill, as if she hadn't been charged for the tea at all; since she hadn't liked it, she was not inclined to argue. She paid and left the bakery, considering her options.

It was pretty plain now what the state of affairs in there was. Not only was there at least one genuine vampire on the premises, but the place appeared to be guarded in some weird way. Something had been determinedly trying to prevent her from smelling anything but the baked goods.

Outside in the snow in the grubby alley, it occurred to Clare that her reaction to the bakery's wares had been a little strange. Cakes didn't normally get her so excited; and the way that she had felt sure that those cakes would be better than *any others in the world* had been decidedly peculiar.

She also realized she hadn't paid nearly as much attention to the bakery's customers as she should have; she could barely call to mind anything about them, although she knew that the place had been full. She slid her phone out of her pocket and thumbed it on. Sure enough, the app was back up, showing the map screen with the blue triangle.

Something inside the bakery must have been jamming the signal as well as interfering with her sense of smell. And that might mean that something more was being hidden there than just one unfriendly Russian vampire. Perhaps she had stumbled upon a whole nest, like the one Jake and Laurence were always boastingly reminiscing about at the office. No, not *stumbled upon*, she thought. Ferreted out. Hunted down. She clenched her teeth as she thought of the months spent listening to Jake and Laurence talk about their hunts, thinking, *How silly, like teenagers reminiscing about a role-playing game*, before she'd been unofficially given the security clearance to learn that not all of the "urban adventures" her company organized were fake.

She noticed something now that she hadn't seen on the way into the bakery. In the window, among the faded newspapers, was a hand-written sign, equally faded: *Room for Rent—Contact Rose.*

On the left side of the bakery, where it was not connected to an adjoining house, a flight of wooden stairs led up to a side door, presumably of a second-storey apartment. That must be where the *Room for Rent* was. Probably the sign was long out of date, and someone had already taken the room. Still, it was worth a try. If she could get above the bakery, maybe her phone could get a reading. She looked down at her clothes, wondering whether there was anything she could do to make herself look like the sort of person who might actually want to live in a place like this. No, she decided. No one who might consider calling a rented room in a Kensington Market back alley home could have afforded her boots. But it wasn't likely anyone here would suspect her motives, either. Thinking ahead, she put her phone in her jeans' pocket, so she would have it on her even if she took off her coat, and climbed the wooden stairs.

The door at the top was labelled, inexplicably, 7C. There was no sign of a doorbell or even a knocker, so Clare hammered soundly with a gloved fist. After a few moments she heard movement inside, then a bolt being drawn back. The door opened, and a blond boy stood looking at her with surprise.

"Hi," she said. "I'm Clare. I'm here about the room?"

"Oh!" The boy's face filled with relief. "Sure. Rose sent you, right? Come in."

He held the door open, and Clare stepped past him into a poky entryway crowded with straggly potted plants.

"So, um … " The boy was looking at her with a kind of nervous admiration. "Welcome to Seven C. Did Rose tell you very much about the apartment?"

"No, she was kind of busy." Was Rose the frumpy pregnant woman? Clare wondered. And did this boy live here with his parents? He didn't look quite old enough be living on his own.

"Well, it's kind of different—oh, you can leave your boots anywhere, it's all right. Um—can I take your coat?"

Clare pushed her boots into a corner and handed over her coat. The boy took Clare's coat gingerly, as if he was afraid he might damage it, and opened two different doors before he found the coat closet.

"The plants are supposed to stop that happening," he mumbled apologetically, to Clare's complete puzzlement. "I'm Nick, by the way."

"Nice to meet you, Nick."

It wasn't, really. Nick was a pale, bony teenager who wore striped pyjama pants with flip-flops, and a greyish T-shirt with *New Moon Soy Sauce* written in red lettering across the chest. His streaky blond hair was longer than it needed to be, and had a tendency to fall in his eyes.

"Well, I'll show you around."

"Sure."

Clare took a surreptitious sniff at the entryway as the boy turned away from her. It was worse than the bakery. The potted plants smelled of nothing in the ordinary way, but when Clare concentrated, all she got was a startling blast of green. That made even less sense than the baking smells downstairs.

"The kitchen is always through here," the boy was saying, bizarrely. "It's one thing you can count on."

Clare forced a slight laugh, as this was probably meant to be some sort of joke. Nick gave her a worried look.

"No, really," he said. "The kitchen is the only room that's always in the same place. It's sort of like the anchor. Everything else moves around."

Clare looked around the kitchen. It was a large, airy room, with windows in places that didn't make sense, considering where they must have been in the house. But everything else about it seemed ordinary: old-looking appliances, cracked flooring, mismatched tea towels, dishes piled in the sink. A big, plain wooden table stood in the middle of the room, with a clutter of what looked like math homework spread out on it.

There was a burst of clicking footsteps, like someone scurrying in high heels, and the door on the other side of the kitchen opened and a small head looked warily in. It was a little boy's head, with dark, curly hair and big brown eyes in an olive-skinned face. It also had a pair of stubby horns.

"Nick?" it said, in a small voice.

"Hey, Yiannis, what's up? Look, this is Clare—she's, um ... She might be our new roommate."

The rest of the boy came around the door. He was wearing shorts, but he was clearly a goat from the waist down, with black, knobby legs that bent in two places and ended in dainty hooves. He also had a little tuft of a tail, which he pulled at nervously while he stood looking up at Clare.

"Hi," said Clare, faintly.

She wasn't quite sure how she was supposed to take this. Frankly, she was dumbfounded. They had never briefed her on ... satyrs? Was that what you called them? She wasn't even sure if anyone in the office knew such a thing existed. As far as she knew, Stake dealt strictly with vampires. But the older boy seemed to expect her to take this in stride, the same way he had expected her to take what he said about the kitchen literally.

"Nick, have you seen Susan?" the satyr boy asked, still looking nervously at Clare out of the corner of his eye.

"Uh, which one is Susan?"

"Susan! My yellow-haired doll. How come you can't remember?"

"You've got so many of them, Yiannis. I don't know where she is. Maybe you put her somewhere and then it got changed around. Why don't you ask Tacky? He can find things."

"He's watching cartoons."

"Well—tell him to stop and help you find your doll. Honestly. He's supposed to look after you."

Yiannis tugged discontentedly on his tail a moment longer, then turned around and clicked back out of the kitchen.

"I'm going to go play on your computer!" he sang out from the hall.

"Don't you dare!" Nick shouted after him. He looked back at Clare and smiled wanly. "He's actually cute, but ... he's kind of bored most of the time, because he can't really go out. He's just living here temporarily—Rose is trying to find proper foster-parents for him. It actually *is* Tacky's job to look after him, but he's basically useless, so ... Um, I should show you the other rooms. Oh, I should mention— you don't have a problem with sunlight, do you?"

"I'm sorry?"

"It's just that the spare room has a big window, and sometimes it's on the front of the house and sometimes it's on the back, so you can't really tell whether you're going to get sun in the morning or in the afternoon. Cristina had that room before, and it used to make her crazy—she couldn't even open the blinds at night in the summer. Right—I'm an idiot. You just came in from outside on a sunny day, so ... "

"I'm not a vampire." It was not something Clare had ever expected to hear herself saying.

Nick smiled. "You totally don't have to say, Clare. That's like ... Rose's thing, kind of. You just don't have to say. It's all good."

He looked at her a moment longer, with an almost reassuring expression, as if he expected her to be comforted by what he had just said. Obviously he was himself. This, to Clare, was the most shocking thing yet. He thought she was some kind of ... some kind of what? A monster, anyway. But it was "all good." He used to live with a vampire; he lived with an orphaned satyr now. He clearly thought Clare had been referred here by Rose because she was some unnatural creature that could find no other place to live. What, Clare wondered, was *he*?

He had gone out through the door Yiannis had come in by, into the hallway beyond, before Clare had a chance to try catching any scent off him. She followed hastily. The hallway was lined with closed doors on both sides, with a last door at the far end. The doors were oddly close together, but even so the hallway looked too long to fit inside one of the narrow row houses that Clare had seen from the alley. It was possible that the apartment might have taken up the second storeys of two houses—but somehow she had a feeling that wasn't what was going on.

"It's bigger on the inside," said Nick, grinning over his shoulder at her. "Do you watch *Doctor Who*?"

"Sorry?"

"Never mind. I just meant—we're still in the same house, but there's more on the inside than the outside. Plus the doors look closer together in the hall than they do inside the rooms. Oh, and it's no good trying to put a sign on your door, or anything. It's not the *doors* that move around."

"Oh," said Clare.

He began opening doors. "Okay … linen closet … Yiannis's room … bathroom—you really have to remember to lock the door."

"I usually do."

"Yeah! I guess that's normal. It's just because … people don't always know it's the bathroom. Some of the doors don't have locks, either, so when the bathroom ends up behind one of those, you have to just shove the laundry hamper in front of it and hope for the best." He opened another door. "Okay, that's Yiannis's room again."

"It's in both places?" In spite of herself, Clare was becoming a little bit curious about how this worked.

"No, it just moved. See, they only move when no one's in them. One time, when I was late for school, I kept getting the linen closet behind every door, and I literally couldn't get to my bedroom. I had to go to school wearing my pyjama pants. It was brutal."

"Wow."

"That doesn't usually happen, though. Plus, Tacky can *kind of* control it. I don't know, he talks to the house, or something." He shrugged dismissively. "Anyway, this is the living room." He opened the door at the end of the hall. "It's always here, too, like the kitchen—it's just not always the same."

The living room looked like something out of the *Arabian Nights*, or maybe the '60s: overlapping, threadbare carpets on the floor, heaps of cushions spilling off awkwardly low couches, hanging coloured-glass lanterns and shelves and shelves of books, with vases and statuettes and candlesticks wedged in among them. There was a television, with a DVD player and a game console, sitting on a coffee table with their cords trailing away behind them to the wall. Draped along one of the low couches in front of the television was a beautiful Asian teenager in jeans and a black V-neck sweater, lazily eating rice crackers out of a Tupperware container with long, slender fingers. It took Clare a moment to determine that he was a boy.

"So the TV is supposed to be for everyone, but if you actually want to watch anything … " Nick gestured towards the couch. "Good luck shifting this bastard."

The boy on the couch waved a remote irritably at the television and pushed himself up onto one elbow. He had silky, waist-length hair that slithered down around his shoulders as he sat up.

"Hi," said Clare, smiling, and then feeling a little foolish. He was obviously much too young for her; but he was just so *pretty*.

He frowned at Clare. "Who is that?" he asked, looking at Nick. He had an incongruously deep voice, and an accent. Oh, *swoon*, thought Clare.

"This is Clare. Clare might be our new roommate. Clare, this is Takehiko. Only, he actually really likes it if you call him Tacky." This was obviously not true.

"Takehiko," Clare repeated. "Nice to meet you. Is that Japanese?"

"Is what Japanese?" He was still giving her a very perplexed look.

"Uh—your name? I just wondered."

Before Takehiko had a chance to answer, Nick, who had walked further into room to look at the television, burst out: "You asshole! Is this a new episode?"

"Yes. Why will I be watching an old episode?"

"You're not supposed to watch any more without me! I thought you promised! Why don't you watch your stupid samurai mecha thing instead?"

"It's finished. I watched all of it."

"Well—couldn't you have waited?"

"No. I like to watch it now. You are busy doing your alchemy homework."

"Algebra, you retard, not alchemy. Aargh! I bet Koga's in this one, too. Koga's my favourite character."

"Excuse me, Stupid—what is she here doing, again?" Takehiko pointed at Clare, who was still standing in the doorway.

"I was interested in renting the spare bedroom," Clare supplied cheerfully.

"Renting?" Takehiko repeated. (When he said it, it sounded more like "Lenting?")

"She means she's thinking of moving in with us," Nick said hastily. "She doesn't literally mean *renting*."

"You have talked to Lo-se?"

"Who?"

"Rose. He means." Nick looked smug. "Hey, Tacky, if she does move in here, you're going to have real fun trying to say her name. *Culll-ay-rrrr.*"

"Please shut up. Rose"—he pronounced the "r" with an exquisite little growl—"did not tell me someone was coming."

"Yeah, well?" Nick countered. "So what? She's busy."

"She would have told me."

"Yeah? Maybe not, you know, because maybe you just lie around watching anime and playing Playstation all day, and so really, why would anybody tell you anything important? I mean, you're supposed to be looking after Yiannis, so how come he's coming to me to ask where his dolls are?"

"Because that is his game. He has hidden the doll somewhere very clever and he wants you to look for it. He has played it with me already all day yesterday. Now he wants to play it with you, but you are too important, you are studying for your important alchemy test, and you are too busy showing girls around the house. Yes." He dropped back onto the couch and pointed the remote at the television. "Go away. They are about to find Naraku's castle."

The younger boy grabbed up one of the cushions and made what looked like a determined attempt to smother Takehiko with it. The Japanese boy pushed him off easily, but he upset the Tupperware in the process. Rice crackers bounced and rolled over the carpet.

"Yahh! Now you make a mess! Stupid!"

Takehiko swung the cushion by one corner and thumped Nick in the head with it. Nick staggered and threw a wild punch that connected with nothing.

"Maybe we should go, Nick?" Clare called from the doorway. "You should show me the rest of the apartment?"

"Oh, yeah—sorry!" Nick clumsily warded off another blow from the pillow. "I'll deal with you later!"

Takehiko dropped the pillow onto the couch and swept his hair back with one hand. Leaving the room, Clare looked back over her shoulder to see that he was still staring after her with a frown. He was almost onto her, Clare thought; or at any rate, he was suspicious. He was obviously smarter than Nick. She needed to get her information and get out of here.

Only what information was she actually looking for now? This whole business had gone well beyond strange already. She had no idea how she was going to put any of it into a report for Seevers.

Nick was now discovering, to his annoyance and obvious embarrassment, that all the doors on the left-hand side of the hall led to Takehiko's bedroom.

"I don't get it—my room has to be here somewhere. And Yiannis wasn't in his room, which means that he was probably in mine, downloading some shit onto my computer—"

"I tell you what," said Clare, taking pity on him and thinking of a way that she might use this to her advantage at the same time. "What if I go into Takehiko's room, and while I'm in there, you open the next door. That way, Takehiko's room can't move—right?"

"Brilliant!" Nick beamed at her. "Wow, Clare, I think you're really going to fit in here."

Ugh, thought Clare. Perish the thought. She stepped inside Takehiko's room and looked around. It wasn't any of the things she had hoped for. It was full of shelves of Japanese comics and elaborate electronics, with posters of spaceships and cartoon samurai neatly arranged all over the walls. A futon was folded tidily in one corner of the room, and next to it a lacquered breastplate, rather like the ones that the cartoon samurai in the posters were wearing, only real and old-looking. And propped next to it was a sheathed sword.

"Clare! I found the room!"

She came back out into the hall, and the door to Takehiko's room swung shut behind her. Nick was hanging out the doorway two doors down. That must mean the one in between was his own room. She guessed it wouldn't look much different than Takehiko's. Probably just messier.

"So ... here's your room—I mean, the room that ... The spare room. It's kind of full of stuff right now. Some of it's Cristina's, that she's just storing here, and some of it's Rose's."

There wasn't much to be seen here. It was an ordinary room, cluttered with the sorts of things that people leave in spare rooms. Since she was supposed to be interested in living here, Clare made a pretence of looking around. Someone—Rose or Cristina—seemed to have a penchant for sunflowers. There were sunflower curtains folded in a pile, and a really awful sunflower clock on top of a rickety chair.

"So how much is the rent?" Clare realized as soon as she had said it that she shouldn't have. Nick had already said something about that. *She doesn't literally mean renting.*

He gave her a funny, worried look. "Rose didn't ... really tell you very much at all ... did she?"

"I meant to ask—but she was really busy."

"Yeah. Um ... well, she doesn't charge us rent. Me and Tacky, I mean. He's been here longer than I have, and I don't know exactly what his arrangement is—he sort of takes care of things around the house. Not that he could really *do* anything else, because he doesn't actually go out. I work for the bakery—that's my arrangement. Cristina too. I mean, she still works there, but now she just gets a paycheque. I don't work in the kitchen—I'm no good at cooking or anything. I do deliveries."

"You mean that bakery actually gets orders from people?"

"Oh, sure. Rose does a good business. There's something about her baking that's irresistible to all kinds of Others. You can tell, right? She doesn't know what it is—it's just like a talent, or whatever. She told me a story about how when she was a little girl she used to make cakes for the fairies in the parking lot behind her apartment building. It started as just a game, only there really were fairies, and they couldn't get enough of her cakes." Nick stopped talking suddenly, and looked at her for a moment with a new, wary expression. "I don't—I don't want to sound like Tacky, or anything, but ... You *did* talk to Rose, right?"

"Of course. Yes. I mean—" Clare decided to go out on a limb. "I couldn't have got in here if I hadn't, could I?"

Nick gave a relieved laugh. "Yeah! You're right! How could you have got in here? Sorry about that! Um ... do you want some tea or something?"

Oh, not tea again, Clare thought disgustedly. What was it with these people and tea?

"Sure," she said. It seemed like the best excuse for lingering in the apartment.

Others. That was what he had said: *all kinds of Others.* You could tell it had a capital O, just from the way he said it. Was that what they called themselves, then? Well, obviously, Clare thought, they weren't going to call themselves "targets"; that was just Stake's terminology.

Something else was bothering her—something that Nick had said. No, she realized, it was what *she* had said, and then Nick had just confirmed it: *How could you have got in here?* How *had* she got in here? She hadn't actually talked to Rose. Except that Rose was presumably the pregnant woman in the bakery, so actually she had … But somehow that didn't seem right.

Clare sat at the kitchen table while Nick put on the kettle and fussed about looking for clean mugs. She tried again to catch some sort of scent. The kitchen would be the logical place, she thought, if it was the only bit of the apartment that didn't shift around. Sure enough, the kitchen was full of scents. Too full, in fact. There was a bright thread of the green scent from the potted plants by the door, and a hint of a sort of old wood smell from the hallway with the moving bedrooms. There was a fairly strong animal smell that she could not quite identify, and there was something else: an old smell, a smell of ink, and rice, and something that she could only describe as magic.

"Tired?"

Clare's eyes popped open. Nick was smiling at her sympathetically as he set a pair of mismatched mugs on the table.

"No, no—well, maybe a little bit."

"I know how it is," he said, looking at the table. "I mean, trying to find a place to live, and … everything. It's pretty hard. Oh—let me get that stuff out of your way!" He reached across to gather up the math homework that was spread out next to where Clare was sitting.

"I guess you're in high school," said Clare. She thought it might be a good idea to remind him just how much younger he was than she, before he tried to take this misguided camaraderie any further. She was beginning to find it tiresome.

"Yeah." He closed the math textbook and began rummaging in a drawer for the tea. "I bet you're wondering why I'm not in class now, right?"

"I suppose you should be."

"Actually it's one of my days off. I go to this alternative school. You only have to go in three days a week, in the morning. The rest of the time you have to study on your own, and stuff—it's hard work. But it's better than a regular school—well, it's the only thing that works for me. At a regular school, you can't pass your courses if you keep missing class, and … if you're like me … you end up missing a lot of class." He had stopped searching for the tea and was now just staring into the drawer. The kettle began to whistle, and he recalled himself to his task with a little start. "Do you want jasmine tea, or Earl Grey, or … something that doesn't seem to have any English on it at all, or—"

"Earl Grey sounds fine," Clare said at random.

"Cool. I'll have that too." He dropped tea bags into the mugs and filled them up. "Anyway, Subway—that's what the school is called, because everybody's always coming and going—anyway, it's great, because this way I can sort of do my own thing when I want, and I still have time to work for Rose, too. I do deliveries mornings and nights. Bread in the morning, cake at night. Here's your tea."

"Thanks."

Clare had been only half listening to him. She had spotted what she thought must be the source of the old ink and rice smell: a painting hanging between two windows on the opposite side of the kitchen. It was one of those long, Asian ink paintings, but it wasn't *of* anything. There were a couple of sprigs of grass in the foreground and a miniature snow-capped mountain with stylized clouds at the very top, but the middle ground was blank, as if it were unfinished. Only it wasn't that, Clare decided. It was as if something had been removed.

"Why do you have a painting with nothing in it?"

"Oh, that." Nick turned to look at it. "That's Rose's. Sort of. It was a gift from a customer, a few years ago. It's actually really old—like four hundred years. I think that's why she keeps it."

"There used to be something in it, before—didn't there?" And Clare thought she could guess what.

"You got it. That's where the bastard comes from. Just the smell of Rose's baking broke the spell, and he got out. It's kind of a shame, really."

"Wow. Four hundred years inside a painting. He seems ... well, he seems fairly normal."

Nick laughed. "If you say so. Actually," he added after a moment, more seriously, "I think he tries ... pretty hard."

Clare sipped her tea, and noticed that the mug said *Fountain of Youth Health Food* on it. So that was the story about Takehiko. She could picture him as a construction of sparse, Asian brush strokes, looking really hot in a kind of stylized way. And he wasn't a target—Other, whatever—after all. She wondered if the fact that he was really four hundred years old could be said in some sense to cancel out the fact that he looked like he was under twenty?

She snapped herself out of that embarrassing train of thought. What was more important than Takehiko's age or relative cuteness was the fact that he didn't seem to quite believe she was really here about the spare room. And when he was finished watching his cartoons (she was not *seriously* attracted to a guy who watched Japanese cartoons?) he would probably go downstairs and ask Rose why she hadn't told him about the new prospective roommate—and that would be that. There was no time to waste.

"Nick, I ... really think that I would like to live here."

"Yeah? That's great! You'd—We'd—It would be great."

"Obviously I have to talk to Rose again, maybe figure out the terms and things. It's just … there's one other thing."

"Yeah?"

Clare looked into her teacup, hoping she could pull this off. It wasn't her usual style. With an effort she called on that special reserve of charm that she had used once or twice before, for quite different purposes and with quite a different type of boy than Nick.

"I guess I've got kind of a thing about secrets," she said. "There've been too many in my life already—I've been hurt a few times too often by secrets." Wow. That actually sounded good. "I know that Rose has that policy where you don't have to tell each other things. It's just … I don't know if I could live like that." She looked up, like a submarine releasing a missile at its target. *Ka-blam.*

"You want me to tell you what I am," said Nick. It was as if he had caught the missile in his bare hands and was just holding it, waiting for it to explode in his face. "Right?"

"I'll tell you about myself. I—"

"You don't have to, Clare. It's okay. I don't mind secrets. But I'll tell you about me. So, um … where do I start?" He smiled awkwardly. "I guess it's best to just say it straight out. Right?"

On the drive home she turned over in her mind the information she'd acquired, wondering what she was going to do about it. Not what she should do, but what she *was going* to do. This happened sometimes; she seemed to see two different possible Clares striding forward into two different futures. In this case, one of them impressed Seevers, showed up Jake and Laurence, got promoted. One was a success.

But the other one, a quieter Clare who was fading into the background now, seemed to feel there was some strong reason not to do all that.

She remembered Jake talking to Kelly, one of the consultants: "Everybody thinks they're a dime a dozen like vampires, but that's bullshit. They're actually pretty rare." And wistfully: "Man, I'd've loved to of seen that."

Yeah, she knew what she was going to do.

"All right, gentlemen—everyone pull up a chair and make yourself comfortable. This is Clare's first pitch, so give her your full attention. She's got something really exciting for us tonight."

Seevers perched himself on the edge of the table in the conference room and winked at her. Jake and Laurence were there, both looking somewhat miffed. The clients, a father and son outfitted in every imaginable piece of Mountain Equipment Co-op paraphernalia, sat grinning delightedly at the far end of the table. Clare felt that the slightly sporty, slightly girly outfit she had changed into for the evening had been well chosen. She was going to do this right. There had been a brief period that afternoon when she had wondered again whether she could do this, whether she *should* do this—but it was past. The little voice that had said, *He's a harmless kid, Clare*, had been silenced, and she was focussed on her goal.

"This is very fresh. You two gentlemen are lucky that you booked with us when you did, because the information that I'm about to give you just became available to us this morning. I was on a routine fieldwork assignment in Kensington Market—I know, not the most glamorous of locales, but very often we find the worst Threats lurking in the strangest places." That was the collective term she'd decided on. It was definitely capitalized, the way she said it. "What I happened upon this morning—" Damn. She hadn't meant to say *happened upon*; she had meant to say *ferreted out*. "Sometimes we talk about 'nests', places where we've found numerous Threats banding together for protection. What I found today is nothing less than a *hive*—a kind of boarding house, an organized enterprise, housing all kinds of supernatural Threats. There is at least one confirmed vampire on the premises. There may be more. There is some other, very strange stuff. There's an underage satyr ... " This drew a laugh from the clients. "There's a four-hundred-year-old samurai who was trapped in a painting. But, for our purposes, most important of all: there's a werewolf.

"Now. Let me explain for you gentlemen who are new to this. Werewolves are a lot rarer than vampires—in cities, *very* rare. But there's more. This particular specimen is what we call a bimorphic werewolf." And by "we" she meant Wikipedia. Nobody at Stake had a clue. "What I mean by that is: he changes form at will." A whistle from the younger client. "That's right. We don't really know much about these beasts. We know there's some kind of compulsion involved—they *have* to spend part of their time as wolves, doing the things that wolves usually do."

"In downtown Toronto?" the elder client burst out.

"Yes, sir. In downtown Toronto."

Preying on the occasional squirrel when he got hungry. Hanging out with a bunch of homeless people who called him Silver and thought he was some kind of dog. Having a hard time finishing high school ... But she had gone over all of that earlier, and dismissed it from her mind. He was a supernatural, capital-T Threat. He was a target.

"Forget what you think you know about the full moon—it doesn't apply. This is the least common, the most dangerous kind of werewolf. And that's what we'll be facing tonight. Now, Mr. Seevers will explain to you our plan of action."

As it turned out, the moon was almost full. It reflected off the snow, giving the night an eerie brightness. Clare locked her car and walked to the library. It was nearly one o'clock, on a weeknight, and the university campus was deserted. It had been a good choice, she thought with satisfaction.

She had been on hunts before, but only as a spectator; tonight she would play a more crucial role. She lingered just inside the library's revolving doors, hands in her pockets. A few industrious students were still here, working on the computers in the part of the library that stayed open all night. She had told Nick that she was a grad student, just because that was what had popped into her head (and because she could imagine some of the graduate students she'd met being undead or inhuman). Then it had provided a good excuse to suggest that he meet her at the library after his night's deliveries were done.

He rode up on an ungainly delivery bike with a big wooden carrier attached to the front. It looked empty. He pulled off his hat and ran a hand through his hair, which promptly fell back in his eyes.

"Hi, Nick!" Clare emerged from one of the revolving doors.

"Hey." He leaned on the handlebars of his bike. "I didn't keep you waiting, did I? I'm a bit late."

"No! It's nice of you to come meet me."

"Sure. Oh, um—" He reached down into the bottom of carrier, and presented her with a small box, tied with string. "Buns. For you." He grinned.

"Aw, thanks—you didn't have to." She opened her purse and stowed the box inside. She would eat those later.

"Well, pretty soon you'll have your own direct supply, right? Anyway, this is just to tide you over. So, where do you have to walk?"

That simplified matters. Clare had not been entirely sure what excuse she was going to give him, but he evidently assumed he was here just to walk her home. She never had told him what kind of inhuman creature she was supposed to be, but he obviously thought it wasn't a very tough one. For the moment that suited her all right.

"I get the streetcar on Dundas, so … "

"Let's go."

They set off down St. George, Nick wheeling his bicycle. He asked about her research, and she made up something on the spur of the moment about studying the portrayal of Others in the media. He seemed impressed. She smirked inwardly.

"Seriously? You can do that kind of thing at university?"

"Oh, sure," said Clare, because for all she knew you could.

"I've been thinking I'd like to apply, once I get enough credits to graduate. I think my grades are good enough, but I don't know if I could afford to go."

"Wouldn't your parents help?" said Clare, for the sake of saying something.

Nick laughed. "You're kidding, right?"

"No … why?"

"Come on, Clare, I thought you were writing your thesis on Others! Couldn't you figure out that I've got six older brothers? We don't all have the same mother—but it's seventh son of a seventh *son* that counts. Anyway, my parents have got *no* money. They couldn't even afford bail the last time Tony got caught jacking a car."

"Oh," said Clare, not totally following that. "That's … um, too bad."

They walked on in silence for a few moments, then Nick said, "You know, if you want, if you're staying late at the library a lot, I can walk you home any time. It's probably not a good idea for you to walk by yourself. I mean—I'm sure you can handle yourself and everything, and I don't mean because you're a girl at all. It's just that I don't know if you know, but there are people—I don't know what, they think they're on *Buffy* or something, but they go on these hunts. There's actually a company that organizes them, called Stake. Apparently it's really expensive, and you basically have to be really rich to afford it. Mostly they go after vampires, because … I don't know, they think that's cool or something. But Rose has heard of dryads getting hunted in High Park. You know what dryads are, right? They're tree spirits—they're totally harmless."

Clare's annoyance had been mounting as she listened to this caricature of her employers, but the bit about the dryads was the last straw. She knew which hunt he was talking about; she'd heard Serena, who organized that one, personally commended by Seevers. Serena had billed them as "wood vampires" or something, and he'd said it was "innovative." Nobody had known they were goddamn *tree spirits*.

"Oh, shut up," she snapped. "You're not totally harmless—you turn into a fucking wolf. And you know what? I'm *so* sick of people comparing Stake to *Buffy the Vampire Slayer*. Stake was founded in 1989. We had the idea before *Buffy*—and Stake isn't some TV show, it's reality. It's real life."

He was staring at her, eyes wide and terrified. "'*We* had the idea ... ' God. Oh, God. That's why Rose hadn't told Tacky you were coming. You're a spy from Stake."

"A *field agent*," Clare corrected him. In a detached sort of way she was amazed by how frightened he looked. After all, she was hardly dangerous.

"And you didn't ... you didn't know about Seven C, before ... Fuck." The expletive sounded almost like a prayer, there was so much feeling in it. "I was the one who let you into the apartment. What have I *done*?"

"I wouldn't worry so much about that," said Clare, surprised. "I'd worry about myself at this point, if I were you."

He looked numbly at her. "Because you're going to kill me, right?"

"No, I'm not." She pulled her purse off her shoulder and dug inside for the papers. "Why would I? What *I* am going to do is get you to sign a waiver, so that *if* the client succeeds in killing you, your family with their seven sons, or whatever, can't sue Stake, because you were a willing participant in a game that went wrong."

"And how are you going to get me to sign that?" he asked, looking at the papers in her hand.

"I'm going to tell you: you can sign this, or we'll raid Seven C." She held out the pen.

"You ... you're going to do that anyway," he said helplessly. "But—I can't just *watch*." He took the pen.

He scribbled a signature on the line that Clare showed him. She refolded the papers and tucked them back in her purse, next to the box of buns that he had brought for her. The street around them was silent and still.

"I'm seventeen, Clare," he said suddenly. "I've never been ... I've never travelled anywhere, or been on a date, or … I don't … I don't even know what else I haven't done—I don't want to die!"

She looked at him. He was pleading with her. The successful Clare noted it with a detached amazement. She wondered if he thought he was talking to the other Clare, the Clare that she had imagined earlier, who had been reluctant to proceed, who'd thought, *He's just a teenager, just a harmless kid.* But how would he know about that Clare? She didn't exist.

"Nobody wants to," the real Clare snapped. "Everybody has to."

Are you sure you can handle prepping the target? Seevers had asked. *Of course,* Clare had said, and meant it. She was a professional; of course she could handle this. It hadn't been hard to get him to sign the waiver, either; a vague threat had been all that she needed. And it wasn't going to be hard to get him to run for the hunters. He was scared. He was crying. He was seventeen; he didn't want to die. *Are you sure you can handle it?* Fuck that! Did Seevers think just because she was a woman, she didn't have what it took? She was going to show him. She was going to show all of them.

"You've got to run," Clare said. "The clients want a chase. They're amateurs—there's always a chance you might get away. So run. It's in everyone's best interest. Jake and Laurence—they're Stake employees. They're out there to make sure the clients get a good hunt. That means they'll try to stop you getting away, but they won't kill you. Honestly, if you get away, it's good for us. One less target we have to locate next time. And werewolves are really rare. I don't know if you knew that. The clients are a man and a boy about your age. They're the ones who are going for the kill."

He was looking at her with desolate, hollow eyes. "Why are you telling me this?"

"Because I want it to look good. This is the first hunt I've pitched and prepped all on my own. Make it look good for me. Okay? Will you do that for me?" She drew off her glove and touched the side of his face. He was kind of a cute kid, after all. Not sexy like Takehiko, of course. But if he *was* going to die, he could at least go with the memory of one kiss.

He slapped her hand away and recoiled with a look of disgust and horror that startled Clare more than anything else that day. The bicycle clattered to the ground and he stepped away from it.

"Watch out, Clare," he said. He looked calm now, but the tears still glistened on his face. "They'll be hunting you next. I don't think you're human."

And he ran. He pelted off down the wide, empty sidewalk, his open jacket flapping as he ran. Clare fumbled for her phone, still stunned by his reaction to her attempted kiss. He had acted as if she were ugly, or something. As if she were an ugly *man*. And when he had said that—*I don't think you're human*—he hadn't meant, *You're one of us.* He had meant: *You're a monster.*

"Jake, it's Clare. We have compliance."

"We can see that," came Jake's voice, dryly.

Jake and Laurence moved out onto the sidewalk, blocking Nick's way. They were both armed with the light crossbows they used on real hunts. Nick turned and ran down a path between two rows of lights on low posts. He had something in his hand as he ran, Clare saw. A cell phone. She should have checked for that, should have confiscated it. Shit.

Laurence had seen the phone too, and shot a bolt that caused the boy to drop it onto the pavement. Jake and Laurence followed him down the path. Clare ran to catch up. By the time she reached the end of the rows of lights, Nick had disappeared from sight, but she could still see Jake, stationed at one end of the area they had chosen as the primary hunting ground. She ran down to join him.

"The fucking kid had a mobile!" Jake had picked up the phone and was holding it in the hand that was not occupied with his crossbow. "And he called someone, too—but it wasn't the cops."

"Where is he?"

"Down there." Jake gestured with the crossbow. "Dropped his coat, for some reason, and kept running. Laurence followed him down, to make sure he doesn't get out the other end. The punters are down around the corner there."

They were standing in front of the physics building, looking down a narrow, enclosed stretch between two buildings, hidden from the street on both sides. There were raised walkways along the edges, beside the buildings, and between them an artfully landscaped strip, now crusted with snow, looking like a small piece of fake tundra. Nick's jacket lay flopped on the frozen grass halfway down. At the far end was a snow-filled fountain basin and a sculpture made of tall poles that glowed mauve at the top. For a moment it was very quiet.

Then there was a noise of running feet and excited shouts from around the far corner of the physics building, and a lean, silver-grey wolf shot out from among the poles of the sculpture to leap over the snow-filled fountain. The clients came storming delightedly after it, brandishing their own crossbows. Laurence jogged casually out after them.

"That was fucking *awesome!*" the son was yelling. "That was better than CGI! Did you see that?"

"I guess they got to see him change form," said Jake, hefting his crossbow into position. "Whatever."

The wolf came racing down the strip of fake tundra, but

drew up short at a couple of warning shots from Jake. It stood there, ears laid back, tail between its legs. Clare could hear it whimpering. It was pretty in a way that Clare had not at all expected. Its fur was glossy and soft-looking, and quite white on its throat and down its legs. Its eyes were a pale yellow-green. She couldn't remember what colour Nick's eyes had been.

The wolf made a move to spring past Jake, but Clare stepped in its path. It stopped, growling slightly. Then it turned and fled.

The clients had got over their excitement at really seeing a werewolf transform and begun shooting in earnest at their prey; but they were both bad shots, and neither knew how to use the crossbows. They chased the wolf up and down the strip of fake tundra, the son running on the walkway by the side of the physics building, the father striding over the frozen grass below. The wolf was very fast, and very agile, and the men were no match for it. But it was trapped in the hunting ground where they had driven it, and it was too scared to make an effective escape. As far as Clare could tell, the hunt was a disaster. There was no way the clients were going to be satisfied, even if they did kill the target. She just wanted it to be over. Finally Laurence, trying to stop the wolf from fleeing past him, either accidentally or deliberately put a bolt into one of its paws. It tried to keep running, but it couldn't. It lay down in the snow. Clare shut her eyes.

Crossbows are quiet; that was why Stake used them. It could have been over already, and she wouldn't know. She kept her eyes closed. She didn't want to know. Only that wasn't true. She wanted it to be too late; she wanted Nick to be dead, because then she could stop thinking about what she wasn't doing to prevent that.

Her eyes snapped open.

"Stop! Stop!" It was the other Clare, who had pushed violently out from somewhere inside her. She was a moment too late to make a difference.

"Holy shit!" came the voice of one of the clients. "What was that?"

The prone body of the wolf was surrounded by blue flame, not as if it were burning, but as if it were enclosed in a flickering blue vessel of fire. As she watched, a bolt from someone's crossbow dissolved into the flame as it reached it. Then she looked up, and saw something dark crouching on top of the glowing mauve sculpture.

It sprang from its perch with the speed of a missile and a dark flutter that was not wings, and it fell upon the younger of the two clients. He gave a choked shriek, and then there was a horrible noise of ripping, and his crossbow fell over the railing with part of his arm still attached to it. The rest of him subsided, groaning, on the walkway, and the thing stood up. It had long claws that caught the moonlight. It leapt over the railing and took down the second client. It evidently had teeth, too. It stood up again, wiping its mouth on the back of its hand. Laurence was feverishly pumping crossbow bolts at it, but they melted into blue flame in the air as they approached.

The thing looked at Laurence, then down at Jake and Clare. It had fiercely yellow eyes, the pupils closed to slits even in the moonlight. Blood dripped from its claws, and it licked its fangs. It was barefoot in the snow, and what had fluttered as it leapt from the top of the sculpture was its long black hair and the black-and-white kimono thing that it was wearing.

"You should have hunted me," it said, in a deep voice with a Japanese accent. "I make a good prey for stupid humans. You could have chased me for a very long time. But not now. You hunted my friend. You will not hunt again."

He sprang at Laurence, batting his crossbow aside as if it were a toy, and caught him by the throat, lifting him off his feet. He drove two claws of his other hand into one eye and then the other, and he dropped Laurence in a heap in the snow. He sprang down the length of the fake tundra to land in front of Jake. He fanned out his fingers in a delicate motion in front of Jake's face. Blue flame sprang out of his palm, and Jake screamed and fell, clutching his eyes.

Takehiko—who was still somehow, horribly, the beautiful teenager from 7C—looked at Clare.

"I did not trust you to begin with," he said. "But I did not think you are so stupid. Do you think that anyone would go to the trouble to seal up a harmless human in a painting for four hundred years?"

And suddenly she understood something about him.

"I know you want to kill me," she said rapidly. Her voice sounded low and husky and not like her voice at all. "And you're right—I'm pretty sure I deserve it. But I think you're going to leave me alive. I think you're going to let me call an ambulance for the others so they don't bleed to death, either. I think you're going to do it because you've got used to living with harmless humans, and you don't want to go back to being what you were before. I think you want to be like them."

Them, she'd said. *Them.* Not *us*.

He looked at her a moment longer, and then he flashed his teeth in a snarl, and turned away.

In the hospital waiting room, Clare listened to Seevers, who had arrived not long after the ambulance, gabbling into his phone about waivers and insurance premiums. This was going to be a disaster for Stake, and she was going to be held responsible. It wasn't fair. She had only ever gone along with the others. She had just been trying to get ahead. It wasn't as if any of this had ever really been her idea. If people wanted to hunt innocent kids who turned into wolves, that wasn't her fault.

She fell asleep in a waiting-room chair, and woke cramped and hungry. She had dreamt of something unsettling, and tried to remember what it was. But no, it hadn't been a dream. She had really done that. She had stood there and waited for Nick to be dead.

But what else was she supposed to have done? If she hadn't been going to do that, why had she done all the work leading up to that hunt? Why had she taken the job with Stake at all?

Threats, she'd said. *Supernatural Threats*. Nick wasn't a Threat, but Takehiko was, that was for damn sure. Compared to him, the vampires that Stake's customers usually hunted were just a minor nuisance, about as dangerous as racoons.

And Nick lived with that thing. Nick made fun of his accent and called him Tacky; Nick had tried to smother him with a pillow. Nick was probably, Clare thought, one of the bravest people she had ever met. And she had tried to lead him to his death, for sport—no, for profit, so that she could profit from someone else's sport, so that she could impress her colleagues and get ahead. And the monster, the real one, had accepted her explanation of his motives—had recognized that she understood him, and left her alive.

In a panic to do something, it didn't matter what, to escape from her thoughts, she reached for her purse on the chair beside her. She remembered the box of buns inside. They would be stale by now. They wouldn't taste the way she remembered that gingerbread, anyway; there was no reason why they should.

She pulled out the box. It was squashed and greasy. Maybe she should eat one, she thought. It would taste like ashes, and that would prove something. She picked out the most squashed, stale-looking bun and bit into it. It was delicious.

It took her two weeks to work up the courage to make the call, and as soon as she hung up, she was sure it had been a mistake. She almost called back immediately to cancel the order, afraid that this was the successful Clare somehow getting the upper hand again. She spent the evening pacing her apartment, waiting for the doorbell to ring. Finally it did, and acting according to the plan that she had worked out beforehand, she ducked into the kitchen and called out, "Come in!"

She heard the front door open.

"Hello?"

She came out of the kitchen, pretty sure from the voice that it was Nick.

It was him, the box of buns she had ordered in his right hand. His left hand was still bandaged where the crossbow arrow had gone through the wolf's paw. He stood frozen inside the door, wide-eyed and white-faced as he realized what he had just walked into.

She held out her hands so that he could see that they were empty, and said quickly, "I want to talk to you. This was the best way I could think of. I had the box with the bakery's number on it."

"Smart," he admitted. He let the door close behind him, wary but not, she realized, actually terrified.

"I wanted to talk to you," she said again. "But you go first."

His chin went up defiantly, and she reminded herself that he was brave, that it was taking bravery for him to face her just then. "I don't have anything to say to you."

"No?" She tried not to sound defiant herself. She wanted to confess, to explain things—but she realized that could easily come out sounding self-indulgent. She wanted him to ask first.

"Well ... " His eyes flicked tensely around her living room, then came back to rest on her. "I guess maybe I do. How did you find Heaven and Earth? That's what we haven't been able to figure out. You didn't just come in by accident, did you?"

"No. We've got—Stake has got an iPhone app. I don't know who designed it for them, but I know it wasn't done in-house."

He goggled at her. "An *iPhone app*? That does what?"

"Maps out locations in the city where ... uh ... I don't know, magic? Where there's a high concentration of magic, or something. I mean paranormal, um ... " she trailed off, embarrassed.

"Yeah, I get it."

"I don't have the phone here—it's a company phone, so ... "

"You don't work for them any more?" He sounded hopeful.

She gave a noncommittal wiggle of her head, neither *yes*

nor *no*. She wanted to be quite honest with him. "I'm on a leave of absence. It's their policy when a hunt goes bad."

"Uh huh. I heard they were basically shutting down."

"No. They're scaling back, but they're not shutting down—they won't be stopping the hunts. But that's not necessarily anything for you to worry about. They're not likely to come after you again, not after the disaster that … Most of them—you've got to understand, most of the hunts are fake. Actors and fake blood, and nobody actually gets killed, unless it's by accident. That's what I was hired to do, organize fake vampire hunts. 'Urban adventures.' They'd been doing it since the eighties. It wasn't until six months ago, when I was promoted, that I found out they did real ones too. And not just vampires—well, you know. Whatever they can find. But until last month, until they got the app, the real hunts were super hard to put together, because they didn't really know where … you … where you guys hang out. And I know the reason they promoted me is because they'd figured out I had what it takes—they knew I'd be good at tracking you down. But why is that?" Here she got to the real reason why she had called the bakery. "What am I?"

He didn't need long to consider that one. "I don't know—maybe you're just a sociopath."

"That's what I've always thought," she said seriously. "When I think about it. But it's not just the lack of empathy. Not everyone can smell … paranormal … uh … magic."

His eyebrows went up. "Yeah, no. That's true. What does it smell like?"

"But surely you can smell it yourself?"

"No, when I'm human I'm just … human. And when I'm a wolf I'm just a wolf. It's actually pretty straightforward." He shifted from one foot to the other. He had started to look intrigued in spite of himself. "You might be … some people have sensitivities. Like … Some humans, I mean."

"Like Rose. That's what you're trying not to say. Like your employer. That's what she is—just human, but with some kind of empathy or sensitivity. That's how she bakes the way she does."

He looked at her like he had a bad taste in his mouth. "You do get why I don't really feel like giving you too much information, right? Because the last time we had a nice frank conversation where I was trying to help you, it ended up with me running away from fucking tourists with crossbows?"

"Yes! I do understand that. That's why I'm trying—that's why I need information. But I do understand. You're right not to trust me."

"Damn straight."

"So that's it. You think I'm just human."

He looked at her for a long moment, appraisingly. "I actually don't," he said finally. "You're probably half human. If I had to guess, I'd say you were probably half fay. That's definitely a thing. And the fay can be pretty sociopathic."

"Half what?"

"Fay. You know. Fairies."

She stared. "You're kidding, right? I'm not a fairy—I'm a monster, some kind of monster. I transform. Like Takehiko. What's he? He's not a *fairy*."

"He's a yokai. A Japanese demon. And he's way outta your league. You just forget about him."

"Sure." She actually took a step back. For a moment there he had looked quite fierce. "I didn't mean … "

He shook himself a little, looking embarrassed by his outburst. "Do you know both your parents?"

"No—my mother left home when I was little, and my father never talks about her."

"Yep, well, I think we solved that one." He put the box of buns down, finally, on the side table by her couch, and stuffed his hands in his pockets. "Look. You … you're not a sociopath. You don't have to be. You didn't let them kill me in the end, and that's great, I'm really grateful. But you were going to, you know? I'm just not ready to be friends right now. Uh … I mean … " He winced. "Not that you necessarily want friends … "

"I do. I want to know other people like me." *Even though other people like me might be terrifying.*

He shrugged, and turned toward the door. "Well, I guess you've got the number for the bakery. You can always try asking for me."

THE SIEGE OF 7C

"SO HERE WE ARE in the pitch dark—all the streetlights have been taken out, and there's no moon. We know there are vampires in the street, but we don't know how many. Then there's the Undead Army moving down University from Queen's Park, so we know we don't have much time, and Maximus is still bleeding *really* bad. Then there's this noise, like rushing water, and it gets louder, and louder—it's coming from somewhere up above us, but we don't know where. And I'm still busy trying to keep the wards up around the perimeter, so it's like—fuck!"

"What did you do?"

"Well, Ranjeet did a Perception roll—and he got a *two*, so Steve was like, 'You can't tell where it's coming from.'"

"Ouch. So what was it?"

"We still don't know. Steve's mom was having some scrapbooking party, and we had to leave."

"Oh, man. That's brutal."

"You've got to come next time, Nick. We *totally* could've used Varcolac yesterday."

"Yeah … if I'm not too busy. You guys have got to game sometimes on nights when I'm not working."

Nick and Ryan were sitting on the couch at Subway, waiting their turns to see the teachers. It was a morning in early March. Nick was sleepy.

"How come you have to deliver cakes at night, anyway?" Ryan asked, stretching out his legs and sinking further into the sagging frame of the couch. "I don't get that—I mean, doesn't the bakery make them during the day? so why can't you deliver them earlier?"

"I just can't. That's the way it's done."

"Well, if you ask me, it's weird."

"Yeah," said Nick. "It's weird." Sure, he thought. Delivering cakes at night was about the *least* weird thing in his life.

Ryan flipped open the dog-eared sketchbook that he always carried around, and clicked his mechanical pencil. The last bit of lead fell out.

"Hey, can I borrow a pencil?"

"Sorry. I've only got a pen."

Nick spotted a familiar figure coming through the front door into the main room of the school.

"Move over, man," he said. "Laura's coming."

"Move over so Laura can sit next to you?"

"Whatever. Move over so she has *somewhere* to sit."

Laura waved from the outer room, where she propped her cane against the wall in order to peel off her winter coat.

"I don't get what you see in her," Ryan muttered. "She's so … mainstream."

"Shut up," said Nick.

Ryan shifted over slightly on the couch, leaving a small

space between himself and Nick. Laura came in and plopped down into it. She smelled of sun and cold air.

"It's nice out!" she announced. "It feels like spring."

"Do you have a pencil?"

"Sure."

Laura fished a pencil case out of her bag and offered it to Ryan. Nick tried to edge his way further into his corner of the couch without seeming like he was trying to move away from Laura—which he wasn't, really.

"Me and Nick were talking about zombies," said Ryan, extracting a fancy-looking red art pencil from Laura's case.

"But we can stop now," said Nick.

Laura smiled and looked interested. She had a nice way of looking interested, Nick thought.

"How are the zombies these days?" she asked, leaning down to put her pencil case away again.

"They're trying to take over Toronto," said Ryan.

"In a Shadow Legions game that we're playing," said Nick, "with some guys from Ryan's old school."

"The school I got *kicked out of*, he means."

"The school Ryan got kicked out of, I mean."

"I see," said Laura. "Is that—Shadow Legions, is that like Dungeons and Dragons?"

"Oh, please!"

"Yeah," said Nick. "Basically."

"It is totally different! For one thing, it's not epic fantasy—"

"Okay, but they're both RPGs—I think that's what she meant. I—I mean, is that what you meant?"

"I don't know." Laura smiled. "Spike used to play Dungeons and Dragons."

"Oh," said Nick.

There was an awkward pause, or at any rate a pause

which felt awkward to Nick. Spike was Laura's ex-boyfriend; it was Spike's motorcycle that Laura had fallen off of two years ago, and that was why she walked with a cane now. Nick was never sure how he should react when Laura mentioned Spike. He wasn't sure whether Spike was currently alive or not.

"His character was a dwarf," Laura added. "That's all I know."

"Dwarves *suck*," said Ryan, sketching busily. "When I used to play DnD, back at my old school, there was this *loser*—"

"Ryan … " Nick tried to interrupt him.

"—who played a dwarf, and—"

"Ryan!" It was a teacher this time, calling from the main room of the school.

"Oh, shit. I am so screwed for this test."

"Good luck, man," said Nick.

Ryan heaved himself up from the couch and shambled off. Laura waved.

There was plenty of room on the couch now, but Laura didn't move over. Nick leaned forward, resting his elbows on his knees. He couldn't think of anything to say.

"You look kind of tired," said Laura.

"Yeah." He smiled. "I guess I am, a bit."

"Up late?"

"Yeah. Working. Then I had a fight with my roommate this morning."

Why had he said that? He was always telling people more than he needed to about himself. You'd think he might have stopped, since two months ago it had almost got him killed; but all that had changed was that now he *noticed* when he was doing it.

"That sucks," said Laura, but she had that interested look

again. It wasn't fake; she really was interested in things. She thought it was interesting that Nick lived in an apartment with a roommate, and had a job that kept him out late at night. She had said so before. Sometimes Nick wanted to tell her about the things in his life that actually *were* interesting. But only sometimes; most of the time he remembered why he didn't.

"What did you fight about?"

"Um, well—I left some towels on the floor. I came in late after work and took a shower, and I was really tired, so I left the towels on the floor."

"That's it? That doesn't sound like a big deal."

"It wasn't." Well. It wouldn't have been, if he hadn't also left his clothes (underwear and all) underneath the towels. And if the reason he had needed to shower in the first place hadn't been … quite so disgusting.

"But he told you off for it?"

"No … that's not really his style. Actually communicating would be too human for him."

Laura laughed. "What did he do?"

"Just acted like an asshole without telling me why."

Laura shook her head sympathetically. "What is up with that? You need to find some new roommates, Nick."

"Yeah, I wish."

"What would it be like if high school were a role-playing game?" Laura asked thoughtfully. "Would we have to roll dice to determine the difficulty of our tests or something?"

"Yeah, probably … and report cards would be like character statistics sheets. *Character Name*: Nick Pereira. *Race*: Human. *Class*: Ordinary High School Student. And you'd get experience points for completing your courses."

"You kind of do. They're called 'credits.'"

"Oh yeah … You may be onto something."

"You think? It would kind of suck as a game, though."

"I don't know. If you weren't an Ordinary High School Student in real life, you might think it was fun."

Laura laughed. They talked about normal things for a while: whether algebra was harder than vectors, why movies based on books usually weren't as good as the books they were based on. Ordinary high school student stuff. And it *was* fun.

But it didn't last. Pretty soon Nick heard his name being called from the main room, and when he had finished that morning's conferences with his teachers, Laura was still writing a test of her own with the math teacher. Nick tried to linger casually, but the only result of this was that one of the teachers noticed him standing around and said, "Nick, you're a friend of Ryan's."

"Uh … yeah." He didn't know what else to say. He guessed Ryan might have said they were friends, though really Ryan didn't know much of anything about him.

But all the teacher wanted was to ask if he would take Ryan's sketchbook that he had left behind.

"Oh. Sure."

He put the book in his bag and then couldn't think of any excuse to stay longer. He took the stairs down and emerged into cold sunlight on Baldwin Street. Laura had been right about the day; it was beautiful. There was a feeling of awakening in the air. For a moment Nick stood with his hands in his pockets, eyes closed, face turned to the sky. He felt like a plant photosynthesizing.

He thought he would sit on the steps and wait for Laura to come down. Then they would have more normal conversation … It would be nice.

His fingers in his pocket encountered the folded shopping list that he had stuffed there on his way out of the house. He sighed, shouldered his school bag, and went to unlock his bicycle from the stand at the side of the school. His weird life awaited.

Some time later, shopping done, he hauled his bags of groceries up the stairs at the side of the Heaven and Earth Bakery, to the door behind which lay the heart of all the weirdness. He had to carry the bags one-handed, because he still couldn't fully close his left hand, the one that had had a crossbow bolt in it two months ago. His keys were inaccessible in his right-hand pocket, so he kicked the door with the toe of his boot instead. After a few repetitions of this, the door was opened by Yiannis, a Barbie doll in one hand and cheese sauce smeared on his face.

"Ohh, he has groceries!" he called back over his shoulder.

"Yeah, and only one useable hand—will you move?"

Yiannis skipped out of the way with a clatter of hooves. "Tacky said it was you," he explained, following Nick across the kitchen, "but I said it wasn't, because you would use your key. I said maybe it was another evil person from Stake, coming to get us!"

Nick dumped the bags of groceries on the counter and looked down at Yiannis, trying to decide whether talking this way meant he was traumatized or just imaginative.

"Well, it was me," he said lamely.

"Yep!" said Yiannis. "Tacky said it was."

"He can usually tell."

Takehiko was sitting at the kitchen table, eating Kraft Dinner with chopsticks and reading a comic with a picture of large-eyed, sword-wielding people on the cover. He might have been deliberately ignoring Nick and Yiannis, or he might have been genuinely absorbed in his reading; with Tacky it was always hard to tell.

"Yiannis, did you ask permission to call him Tacky?"

"No."

"Then maybe you shouldn't."

"That's what you call him."

"Yeah, but … that's different."

The little satyr looked sceptical. "Why?"

"Just because, okay? I don't suppose you guys saved any KD for me." He looked in the pot on the stove, and saw that it had been scraped clean.

"Ta-ke-hi-ko said you don't like it."

"No, I don't," said Nick angrily, "but I did want something for lunch. For fuck's sake. I just did the grocery shopping—*all* the grocery shopping, *as usual.*"

He strode over to the table to glare down at Takehiko. Somehow looking at him made Nick even angrier. For someone who didn't leave the house, Takehiko dressed unnecessarily well. He had on a cherry-red sweater that Nick personally would never have dared wear, and jeans with a lot of unnecessary pockets. He looked like he was dressed to go to a club, or hang out at the mall, not sit around the house reading manga.

"Hey!" Nick found he had snatched Takehiko's comic out of his hand without really thinking about it.

He was repaid with a ferocious glare. "What?"

Takehiko's hair was pulled back in a ponytail, so that his ears showed. Even in his fully human form, the tops of his ears were slightly pointed. Nick thought this was an affectation.

"I've just been out getting the groceries, and you guys didn't save me any lunch?"

Takehiko got up from his seat and stalked across to the counter. He picked up a plate which, Nick saw to his embarrassment, had a sandwich on it, and turned back to Nick.

"My book," he said, holding out his hand. Nick surrendered it. "Your sandwich." He presented it with a slight bow.

"Thanks," Nick muttered.

Takehiko went back to the table and picked up his chopsticks again. Nick sat down with the sandwich. It was a bacon, lettuce, and tomato sandwich, made with slices of Rose's bread, perfectly toasted and still just warm. It looked delicious. It *was* delicious. Nick felt very, very bad, and didn't like it.

He waited for his moment, when Takehiko set down his comic briefly to reach across the table for the ketchup.

"I'm sorry you had to clean harpy shit out of the bathroom this morning."

"Mm." Takehiko nodded, and squeezed ketchup onto his Kraft Dinner.

"You're still mad, aren't you?" said Nick after a moment.

"No." Takehiko set down the ketchup and picked up his comic again.

"You look like you're still mad."

Finally Tacky looked at him across the top of the comic. "I can get mad again," he said. "But this is just how I look."

Nick finished his sandwich in silence. What did he care whether Takehiko was mad? It had been an honest mistake, anyway, leaving that stuff on the floor. It had only happened because he had been tired from doing his job. And taking care of the apartment was Tacky's job, after all.

Yiannis had finished his Kraft Dinner by this time, and was sitting under the table enacting some sort of soap opera with his Barbie dolls. Then the phone rang, and he bolted out and skittered across the kitchen to answer it. Of course it wasn't for him; he just liked answering the phone.

"Nick!" he announced, holding out the receiver and balancing on one hoof. "It's for you!"

It was Nick's father.

"I'm just calling to see if you're all right," he said, sounding as awkward as usual.

"Yeah … " Nick leaned one shoulder against the fridge, pulling the phone cord as far as it would go. "I was waiting for you to call."

"Oh?"

"I saw it on TV—that woman in the park … "

"Ah."

"Every time there's a murder, you call to ask if I'm all right. God, Dad—how many times do I have to tell you? I don't kill people. Watch the fucking Discovery Channel or something, why don't you? Wolves only hunt large prey in packs, okay? I don't have a *pack*. Fuck—I don't even have *friends*!"

"Nicolau, I'm just—"

He banged the receiver down and slumped against the fridge, wondering miserably how it was that he had got so mad.

It was very quiet in the kitchen. Yiannis was back under the table, combing the hair of one of his Barbies with his fingers. Takehiko seemed to have finished his comic.

"I'm going out," said Nick.

He tore down the stairs, not even bothering to close the front door behind him. He had to cling to his human form from the inside. The feeling made him sick to his stomach. He pounded down the alley and out into the market, thinking only of his goal.

In his cold, cramped hiding place, he dragged his sweatshirt over his head in one motion, kicked off his sneakers and fumbled desperately with his belt buckle. His other self, always almost there like a snarl at the back of his throat, rose out of him before he had quite got out of his jeans. He shook himself free of the weight of cloth, lashing his tail, and circled about, looking for the pale, discarded form of the human boy that he had somehow just been inside. As always, there was no sign of him. This never failed to puzzle the wolf.

But he was a wolf, and he didn't stay puzzled about things for long. He shook himself a little, squeezed out of his hiding place, and limped off into the cold, bright afternoon.

There was a memory that he held carefully, like a fragile thing, in a corner of his mind. (It was Nick's memory, nothing to do with the wolf, who didn't really understand why it was important.)

In the memory, Nick woke, and realized that he had woken, and that made him so happy he felt like crying. It was that strange, still time of the early morning, when the sunlight makes everything look new. Of course, he was in the living room, where the furnishings moved around and changed colour subtly while you weren't looking, so things often looked new.

He looked up at Takehiko, who was still asleep, his head resting on his arm on the back of the couch, his shiny hair spilling down over the pillows. He had changed into pyjamas at some point in the previous night, because the black-and-white yukata had got blood on it. He looked pretty harmless now. Pretty cute, too, actually, said a part of Nick's mind that he usually did not listen to. He was listening to everything right now; it was so good still to be able to.

Another part of his mind was wondering how it was that he could even look at Takehiko right now, after watching him tear into those people last night. Of course, he had looked a lot more like a yokai then than he did now. Nick didn't think he had actually killed them, and wasn't totally sure he would mind if he had. Maybe it was just that you couldn't look away from someone who had done that kind of thing for your sake. You would be worse than Clare.

But that wasn't it, really. As far as Nick could remember, he had never heard Takehiko call anyone his friend. And he, Nick, had certainly never had a friend who would come looking for him on the basis of a phone call that only rang once, and find him, too, and then chew on people just because they had hurt him. So what if he was also kind of a bastard who pretended not to know the difference between alchemy and algebra, and watched ahead in shows without waiting for you?

Takehiko had opened his eyes. They were brown again.

"Hey," said Nick. "Why have I got my head in your lap?"

"I don't know. You fell asleep like that." He stretched and yawned, shaking back his hair. "You licked my face, too. It was disgusting."

Nick remembered that, vaguely. He started to sit up, and looked down at himself. He was covered up with the crocheted afghan, which was all shades of orange and brown this morning, but other than that he was naked.

"Oh. Uh. Weird. I don't usually change in my sleep. Maybe it was stress or something."

The bandages on his hand were—well, they were on his hand now, instead of the wolf's paw. Somebody must have taken care of that, too, while he slept. He remembered Rose the night before, when Takehiko came back carrying him, how she had been so angry she had to make an effort to calm down enough to be comforting.

Nick sat up all the way, pulling the orange-and-brown afghan up around his shoulders.

"You saved my life, Taki. I don't know how to thank you."

Takehiko gave him one of his long, uncomprehending looks. "Why not? That was good."

"Thank you for saving my life, Takehiko."

"You're welcome." He slid off the couch and began rummaging through the DVDs that had been deposited in a heap on the floor when the big, glass-topped coffee table had changed into a tiny Ikea TV stand. "So what is the last episode that you saw, again?"

"Um … Kagome and Inuyasha were fighting, or something, and—do you think I could have breakfast first, please?"

"Mm." After a moment he put down the DVD and got up. "I will make you some toast."

And that was it.

It was dark when Nick came back to the bakery. He let himself in by the back door, and found Cristina cleaning up in the kitchen.

"Rose isn't finished packing the cakes yet," she informed him. "A lot of customers come in at the last minute, so we can't close yet. So inconsiderate! Do they think we do not have lives?"

Nick made some sympathetic noise and restrained himself from saying, "Maybe they've noticed that you're undead." As far as he could tell, Cristina did not have a sense of humour.

In the front of the bakery, Rose was leaning against the counter, listening to a regular, a woman named Anita, complain about the Office of Other Affairs.

"Of course they are underfunded, and of course they are

ineffectual," Anita was saying. "But the whole idea was absurd to begin with. We lead secret lives—having a government agency 'in charge' of us, without the general public or the rest of the government *even knowing* is ridiculous."

"I see your point, but I think Other Affairs does some useful things." Rose saw Nick hovering in the kitchen doorway and waved.

"Hello, Nick!" said Anita.

"Other Affairs has been pretty good to Nick," said Rose. "They paid for him to go to Dr. Kumar after he got hurt recently."

"Really? But Nick has a human identity, and he was born here, wasn't he? Surely he has a health card?" She looked at Nick. "Don't you?"

"Yeah, but ... Dr. Kumar is a vet."

"Right." Anita nodded. Nick wasn't sure whether she knew he was a werewolf; but most of the people who came into Heaven and Earth just took these things in stride. "And how's Takehiko?"

"He's good," said Nick, since the question had been directed at him.

"I heard he was involved in that ... bad business in January."

"Yes," said Rose. "They put him on the Dangerous Subjects list afterwards. But all that means is that he has to report his whereabouts, and that's not cramping his style very much."

"Still—" Anita would obviously take any opportunity to criticize the government. "He can't have taken that very well!"

"Oh, I think he was flattered." Rose grinned. "He likes being treated like a human."

"That's being treated like a human?"

"Oh, yes! Bureaucracy is very human."

Nick retreated into the kitchen, in case they were going to go on talking about Tacky. He managed to stay out of Cristina's way and avoid being put to work until Anita left and Rose came back to the kitchen. Cristina went out to lock up and tidy the front of the shop.

"You're looking well, Nick," said Rose.

"Am I?" It worried him to hear things like that when he wasn't aware of looking any particular way.

Rose shrugged. "You always come back looking good when you've been ... out. It must do you good."

"Yeah, I guess. Are these leftovers?" He pointed to some buns on the counter.

"Go ahead. That's not your dinner, though, is it?"

"No, I ate already."

Rose looked at him a little warily. He swallowed the bite of delicious pastry that he had already taken.

"Leftover jerk chicken. Some Jamaican guys were eating takeout in the park, and they thought I looked hungry."

"I see," said Rose. "It must be something about you."

"Huh?"

"People feel like feeding you. Takehiko told me you ran into some harpies last night."

"He did? Oh. I didn't, really. I just came across a nest. It was down at the Harbourfront, on the roof of one of Ivan's clubs. I don't know if it was abandoned or not—I got out of there pretty quickly. I called Ivan to tell him about it. But I fell down on the way out, and got ... made a mess of myself."

"Well, that's good—I mean, I'm glad that's all it was. You should tell Takehiko that. I think he was worried."

"*Worried*?" How could you tell? Nick wondered. What would that even look like?

"Nick ... "

"Sorry. You're right. I should have told him."

"Well, anyway. I told you before that I'm going to be gone tomorrow?"

"Yeah. Will Cristina be in charge again?"

"No … That didn't go very well last time, so we decided I'd just close up for the day. I'll put up a notice saying I'm out of town."

"Right." He wanted to ask where she was going, but Rose always said you didn't have to give details, and he figured that must apply to her too.

He loaded up his delivery bike, then ran upstairs to duck in the door of 7C and get his coat. He remembered Ryan's sketchbook, and thought he might return it on his route, so he grabbed his school bag at the same time and slung it over his shoulder.

The night was gorgeous, the air silkily cool, the sky not yet quite black. Nick rode with his coat open, pedalling the heavily laden bike in time to a song that was running through his head, one from In Principio's new album.

He made the local deliveries first. The cake boxes all had labels taped to them with the address and delivery instructions. He climbed a fire escape behind an old apartment block and left a box on the ornamental ledge that ran around the top of the building. He knocked three times at a garage door in an oddly shaped building covered in graffiti, left a stack of boxes, and pedalled away without looking back. He made several stops in small, unexpected urban parks, where he left cake boxes on benches and behind trees. Most of the cake deliveries were to regular accounts who settled up with Rose periodically, or paid for their cake with something other than money. In some places he collected payment himself. In one park a woody-looking person solemnly counted out a heap of shiny pebbles into his cupped hands. At a basement door he received a wad of crumpled bills from a giggling girl with wings. Sweet, unsettling music and soft voices curled out of the room behind her, and Nick asked if she was having a party. She giggled harder and nodded.

"Have fun," he said. "Enjoy the cake!"

He rode back to Kensington, skimming along now on a drastically lightened bike. He let himself in by the back door again, picked up the rest of the night's orders from the dark bakery kitchen, and set out on the Paths.

In Nick's weird life there were only a few things that still gave him that cold, pit-of-the-stomach feeling of facing something really alien. The Paths were one of them. He didn't know what their technical name was, or if they even had one. They were Other, but they were not open to just any Others. They belonged to the Sidhe, and Rose's employees were allowed to use them only in return for supplying the local courts with baked goods. Nick was not allowed to go on the Paths except when he was on a delivery; it wasn't that he *couldn't* have, but Rose had told him very firmly not to.

"Just think of the Sidhe as the mob," she had said, "and you won't be far wrong. You *don't* want to owe them anything."

At night, almost any empty arch or gate opened onto the Paths. You just had to know how to walk through it. Nick wheeled his bicycle to the wooden gate that stood open at the end of the alley, behind Fountain of Youth. He swung one leg over the bike's seat and walked slowly through.

He was not Nick Pereira, ordinary high school student. He was Nick Pereira who was also a wolf. He let the snarl of his other form rise up in him until for a split second he was looking out of his human body with the wolf's eyes, and then the path opened in front of him and he shoved the bike through.

He let out his breath in a slow sigh, spun the pedals, and let the bike coast. It was always like going downhill on the Paths, no matter which way you travelled, although it looked like level ground.

He wondered, not for the first time, what it looked like when he hit that state that allowed him onto the Paths. He wondered if his eyes actually turned yellow and … what was the word? Lupine. He realized that he knew roughly what that would look like. Takehiko's eyes that night had been very yellow.

He opened his own human eyes again and concentrated on where he was going. You couldn't navigate on the Paths, but you had to be very sure about where you were headed, or you would never get there.

Looked at out of the corner of your eye, the Paths looked like the inside of a concrete tunnel, with lights passing by on either side. There was a loud, faraway sound of water, and a wind. But you weren't anywhere. Somehow Nick had always known that. And it wasn't a good idea to look at the walls, because they weren't really there either.

Nick rode the Paths three nights a week, and he was used to them by now. Once you stopped being scared, they were fun. He took his hands off the bike's handlebars and held out his arms so that his coat billowed back in the wind. He had never met anyone else on the Paths; he thought probably you never did. He knew without being told, though, that it would not be a good idea to sing.

Once you'd been on the Paths once in a night, it was easier to get back on them. Nick got off at his furthest destination—some park in Ajax—and worked his way back from there, scooting on and off the Paths now without having to pull out his wolf form the way he had at first. Some of the exits were more convenient than others. Parks often had gates or arches which served the purpose, but when his destination was a house or a building, he would often get off a few streets away and find the place in the normal way.

Of course with the Sidhe deliveries it was a different story. The Paths would deposit you on their doorstep, if not actually inside their court. There was only one Sidhe delivery tonight, one of the last ones. It was a special order from a visiting court, and the address, on Church Street, was unfamiliar. Nick rode off the path to find himself in the lobby of a stately old apartment building.

He backed his bike hastily out the doors into the real world, and bumped it down the steps to lock it to a bike stand outside the building. He always tried to be on his best behaviour with the Sidhe. He checked his person hastily for bits of metal that might be iron. His belt buckle was something bronzy, so he thought it was probably okay, but he wasn't so sure about the buckles on his school bag. To be safe, he stuffed it down among the remaining items in the bike's half-empty barrow after he had extracted the cake boxes for this address.

Back inside the building, he rode up in an elevator with mirrored walls concealed behind grubby quilted curtains. The elevator was very slow, and long before it reached the sixth floor, Nick had become convinced that there was something else behind the quilted curtains besides mirrors. It wasn't entirely unlikely.

He got out of the elevator with some relief, and knocked on the door of Apartment 612. It was opened by a person with long, pale hair and oddly fishlike grey eyes.

"And what would you be wanting?"

"I've brought your cake."

"You're not one of the Folk, are you?"

"No." After a moment's silence, Nick decided they weren't going to get anywhere until he said what he *was*. "I'm a werewolf."

"A werewolf baker?"

"No, just a delivery boy."

Since it was a Sidhe delivery, even though it was a special order he didn't have to stay for payment; but this group of Sidhe wanted to give him a tip, and insisted that he come in while they looked for it. He would really have preferred not to. They seemed to be having some sort of party. A bachelor party, maybe, he would have said if they were human. At least he *thought* they were all male. They were all kind of like Irish versions of Takehiko: pristine and young and kind of girly, but obviously human only on the outside. They were also, he had to admit, meaner than Takehiko.

"Answer me a question, Werewolf," one of them said, beckoning him over to a window. "I find it so hard to tell these humans apart. Do you see those two walking past, holding hands? Which one is the man and which the woman?"

Nick looked dutifully down at the couple, but he already knew what he was going to see. They were on Church Street. Both halves of the couple were broad-shouldered and bearded.

"Those two are, um ... both men."

"*Are* they?" said another Sidhe who had come up beside them.

"Yeah. Um ... you'll see a lot of gay couples in this neighbourhood. It's ... the, uh ... Gay Village."

"They are *holding hands*."

"Yeah."

"Why?"

"Uh … they're gay."

He looked around the room. Everyone seemed to be interested by this time. This isn't happening, he thought. You guys are *fairies*. I can't be explaining "gay" to a room full of *fairies*.

But he was. "It's, um … when two guys are attracted to each other, and then, when they're a couple, like a man and a woman—or it could be two women … " He realized he wasn't making any sense.

"Do you mean to say there is more to it than holding hands?"

"Yeah, like … sex and stuff." There was a horrible pause. "It's—it's—pretty okay. I mean, there's nothing wrong with it."

"Truly? Then why are you turning red like that?"

"A-am I?" He knew that he was. "I don't know … "

"Maybe it is because there aren't any gay werewolves. Would that be true?"

"Yeah," Nick said readily. "I think so."

It was a lie; he had no idea whether there were gay werewolves or not. But it got at a truth, which was that even if there were, they had nothing to do with him.

"Pity," said one of the fish-eyed Sidhe.

"Yes, I rather think they're missing out," said another.

Of course they knew what "gay" meant. They knew what Church Street was about, too. Some of them were planning on going out to a bar later, "to pick up some mortal boys." They had been teasing him. Nick tried to pretend that he had known this, and that he didn't really mind, but he knew he did a very bad job of it. Finally they decided to be merciful, or grew tired of their joke, and let him leave.

"But it has been an *eye-opening* experience," said one of

them, holding the door for him. "I hadn't met any of your kind before."

"Nor I," said the long-haired one who had let him in. "To tell the truth, I would have expected a werewolf to be more ... butch."

"Fuck you, Legolas," Nick muttered to the closed door.

He took the stairs down to the lobby, still feeling the blood throbbing uncomfortably in his face. The Sidhe had given him a large tip in very shiny coins, but he fully expected them to have turned into something else by the time he got outside. He was not wrong; when he opened the front door to retrieve his bike, he found he was holding a handful of little plastic packets marked *Leaf Brand Condoms: Berry Flavour*. Only a strong disinclination to litter prevented him dropping them on the spot. Instead he shoved them distastefully into his jeans' pocket. Then he saw what had happened to his bike.

It was surrounded by pigeons. They had got into the barrow on the front and torn open a box of cake, and they were flapping around, eagerly eating. Somehow they had tossed his school bag out, and it had burst open. Ryan's sketchbook lay on the pavement, torn pages ruffling in the breeze.

And it had seemed like it was going to be such an uneventful night. A small crowd had gathered, at a wary distance, to watch the spectacle. Once it became obvious that it was Nick's bike, a couple of people stepped up to help him. A man in leather pants helped to shoo the pigeons away, which took a surprising amount of work. They would flap away from the bike and then land a short distance away and immediately start waddling intently towards it again.

"Nice pictures," said a woman with spiky hair, handing Nick back the remains of Ryan's sketchbook. "Too bad it got wrecked."

"Thanks. It's not mine. It belongs to a friend."

"Shit," she said sympathetically.

"I think that's got rid of them," said the man in leather pants.

"Thanks."

"It was kind of a weird thing—I was on the other side of the street, so I didn't quite see what happened, but ... it was like some kind of pigeon explosion—wings everywhere. What have you got in there? Some kind of pigeon crack?"

"It's just cake," said Nick.

"Well, good luck."

Reluctantly, Nick dug into the bicycle's barrow to assess the extent of the damage. There had only been two cake boxes left, and both had been breached and their contents thoroughly pecked. He fished out the delivery slips. One had a number, so he called it, and explained that there had been an accident and tonight's delivery would not be coming. The customer gave a horselike snort, called him incompetent, and hung up. Nick noticed that there were still pigeons loitering around the front of the building, watching him with small red eyes in the darkness. He looked grimly down at the boxes of pecked cakes. He would have liked to dump the things in the nearest garbage, but with Rose's baking that wasn't safe. He had to take them home to dispose of them properly.

The last delivery address was a park, but the cake was supposed to be paid for on the spot, so Nick decided he ought to go there and explain what had happened. At this point it seemed only fitting that when he tried to get back on the Paths, he couldn't. They seemed to need him to prove himself again, and he just didn't have it in him any more. That fairy had been right; he never looked the part, and right then he didn't feel it either. He pedalled wearily on his way.

He got lost, and it took him nearly an hour to find the park. He kept being distracted by fluttering noises behind him or pigeons suddenly flapping up in front of his bike. They would not leave him alone. He wasn't even sure what pigeons were doing up at this hour. It was well past midnight. Shouldn't they be sleeping so as to greet the dawn or something?

He found the park at last, and had a confusing conversation with a slimy, lisping head that poked out of a drain. Once they succeeded in understanding each other, the slimy head was much more sympathetic than the other customer had been. It didn't seem bothered by the idea of eating cake that had been pecked by pigeons, either, so Nick gave it both its own order and the other pecked one. It paid with something in a little leather pouch that smelled of dirt.

He hoped the pigeons would leave him alone now, but they were still following him as he cycled home, flapping and waddling at the edges of his vision. He was past caring by this point. By the time he reached 7C he could barely keep his eyes open. There was light under the living-room door, which probably meant that Tacky was still up, playing Playstation or watching TV or something. These days Tacky was often up when Nick got in at night, and Nick would usually put his head in the living-room door to announce that he was back, although he knew that this was unnecessary. Tonight he didn't bother. He made a vague attempt at brushing his teeth, found the door to his room on the fourth try, and fell into bed.

The world was grey and cold. There was a noise, a kind of flapping and bumping, and a loud, insistent warbling: *wuuuu-wuuuu, wuuuu-wuuuu* … It was because of the war, but it was okay, the government would take care of it … if only they had enough Gatorade. Nick rolled over and tried to pull the covers back up over his shoulder. He had got them tangled up somehow, and he was lying on something uncomfortable … It was his belt. He had gone to sleep wearing his jeans. This realization was what woke him. He pushed himself up onto one elbow and rubbed his eyes.

The clock beside his bed read 7:13, and Takehiko was standing in his doorway. He had a mug of tea in his hands, the steam still rising from it. His blue yukata was loosely belted and open down the front, almost to his waist. He wasn't looking at Nick, but at something beyond him, outside the window. Nick wondered how he could have compared Takehiko to those ridiculous Sidhe the night before. They were nothing alike, really.

"Hey … mm … bakery's closed today. Forgot to tell you. Didn't have to wake me."

"I didn't wake you," said Takehiko. "Look."

Nick twisted around to look, and then backed away so violently that he fell off the bed altogether, dragging the tangled bedclothes with him. The noise of flapping and loud warbling was coming from the window above his bed, which was full of pigeons.

It was a casement window with a screen on the inside, and it had been open slightly when Nick went to bed. Three pigeons had crammed themselves into the space between the windowpane and the screen, and squatted there, making smug *wuuu-wuuu* noises, while dozens of other birds flapped and circled and bumped against the window in a confusion of grey feathers.

"They are all around the house," Takehiko said. "Every window is the same."

"Oh, shit," said Nick.

"Mm!" Tacky closed one thin hand into a fist. "I knew this is somehow your fault."

"It is *not* my fault!" Nick picked himself up from the floor, kicking free of the bedclothes.

"Oh, it is not? What is *Oh, shit*, then?"

"It's … rrgh … " Nick scrubbed his hands roughly over his face and through his hair. He looked briefly at the window and then away again. "Some pigeons followed me home last night, okay? Look, I'll tell you the whole story, but will you give me a minute to get dressed?"

Tacky nodded and went out, sipping his tea. The door swung shut behind him. Nick found a relatively clean T-shirt on his floor and pulled it on. He knelt on his bed and reached warily for the crank of the casement. The pigeons stared at him through the screen with mad red eyes. He gave the crank a twitch, hoping to scare them into flying out. But they only flared their wings and cooed louder. Then he tried opening the window further, but this was a stupid mistake; two more pigeons got in, and began pecking at the screen. Nick retreated to the kitchen.

Takehiko was sitting at the table. There was another mug of tea waiting for Nick. He slid into his chair and rested his head in his hands.

"So. Please tell me how this is not your fault."

"Okay … " Nick did his best to explain what had happened after he left the Sidhe apartment building the night before. "It did occur to me that it was weird," he finished, "but I swear I didn't see this coming."

The kitchen was twilight-dark, and they had to speak in raised voices. All the windows looked out onto masses of flapping, cooing pigeons.

Takehiko nodded. "I think you are right. This is not your fault."

"Well, thanks." Nick took a swallow of tea. "What are we going to do? Rose is away, too."

"Mm. Visiting her mother."

"Really? How do you know?"

"She said."

"Oh." So she told Tacky where she was going, then, but not Nick. He felt irrationally irritated by this.

"We can call her, I guess," said Tacky doubtfully.

Nick thought briefly about how much he would like to have anyone from 7C or Heaven and Earth calling him when he was at his parents' house. "Let's not," he said.

"We don't want to bother her," Tacky agreed. "We will get rid of them on our own—"

"And then we can tell her about it—or not—when she gets back."

"Yes. That is a good idea."

They sat and drank tea for a few moments in perfect agreement.

"That's messed up," said Nick presently. "How can they be at the windows on that side? Those windows aren't actually on the outside of the house."

"I know. I noticed this too. They have got inside the house's magic somehow. It is strange—we can only think that they followed you home because they want more of Rose's cake. But it was only a few pigeons who ate the cake to begin with." He shook his head. "They cannot be ordinary pigeons who just want cake."

"Could they be a curse or something? Rose might have enemies."

"Yes, she has enemies. But I do not think they would send pigeons."

More stuff that he knew about Rose! It pissed Nick off. He was on the point of saying something unwise about it—*I suppose you know who the father of her child is, too,* or something like that—when they were interrupted by a shriek from the hall.

Takehiko was out of his chair, across the kitchen, and through the hall door before Nick had even pushed his chair back from the table. When Nick got there, Takehiko was backing out of a doorway full of flapping grey wings, holding a pyjama-clad Yiannis under one arm.

"Oh, no," Nick moaned. "What did you do?"

Tacky banged the door shut and set Yiannis down.

"I just opened my window!" Yiannis crumpled to the floor, black goat legs splayed, and began to cry.

"Little brother, it's all right." Takehiko squatted beside him. "You did not know they were going to come in."

"Yeah, it's not your fault," Nick chimed in feebly. "I didn't mean that."

The noise of flapping and cooing had moved off down the hall, switching from one door to the next, as if the apartment was doing its best to get rid of the pigeons. But it wasn't working.

"They're still coming in," Nick observed.

"Yian-chan, I need you to do something. I'm going to open the door again, and then I want you to think of home. Okay?"

"Okay," said Yiannis tearfully.

Takehiko scooped the little satyr up again, and slapped his free hand on the nearest door.

"Come here please," he said. "Calm down. *Daijobu desu*."

To judge by the noise, the room full of pigeons had stopped on the other side of the door where Takehiko had his hand. He reached for the doorknob.

Yiannis let out a howl as the door opened onto his bedroom, every piece of furniture and inch of floor hidden under a carpet of pigeons. They weren't the tidy, soft grey kind of pigeons, with striped wings and iridescent green around their necks. They were the foulest, dirtiest pigeons Nick had ever seen, the kind of pigeons that look like they have bathed in garbage and carry all the diseases known to man. The smell was ghastly. More pigeons were still swooping in at the open window, circling through the air, and jostling the others as they looked for a place to land. And they had seen the open door …

Yiannis screwed his eyes shut, and a light seemed to go on in the room. The pigeons outside the window were gone, and a beautiful view of wooded hills standing out against glittering blue water had replaced them. But the foremost pigeons in the room were already starting to flap and waddle out into the hall.

"No, no! Get away!" Yiannis yelped, squirming in Takehiko's grip.

"It's okay, Yiannis," said Nick. "They're just pigeons."

"They tried to peck out my eyes!"

"It is all right," said Takehiko calmly, "we are going." He held up a hand, and the pigeons started back from a sort of curtain of blue flame that sprang up across the hallway.

They returned to the kitchen. Yiannis, past the worst of the shock, was now crying miserably for his pigeon-infested room and his dolls.

"They're going to shit all over them!" he sobbed.

"Shh-shh. We will clean it up if they do."

Takehiko had wet a dishtowel and was gently trying to wash the scratches on Yiannis's face and arms. It really did look like the pigeons had attacked him. Nick stood by the table, feeling useless.

"Nick doesn't even care!" Yiannis added, his face crumpling up again. "Nick's not even our friend!"

"What?"

"He said so yesterday. He said, *I don't even have friends*! He said that!"

"Ohh—yes, but he did not mean us." Tacky moved to sit on the floor next to Yiannis, arms around his knees.

"He meant *everybody*—hello?"

Takehiko shook his head. "No, he didn't mean us, though. You can tell that he is our friend. He buys us food and things."

"That's just because he has to."

"I don't think so."

Yiannis slid his hooves about on the slippery kitchen floor. "Why did he say that, then, about not having friends?"

"I think … Ah! I think because he is a teenager."

"Uh … what are you?"

"I'm a five-hundred-year-old demon."

"Oh." Yiannis looked at him a moment longer, then up at Nick. He had apparently forgotten about crying. "I always thought Nick was the oldest."

"Nope," said Nick. "Not really."

"I'm still not talking to you," Yiannis said primly. "Even if you are a teenager."

Takehiko got to his feet. "What do you want for breakfast, Yian-chan?"

"Corn Pops!"

"*Hai.*" On his way to the cupboard, Takehiko paused to look Nick in the eye. "Stupid. Bastard."

"I'm sorry, okay?"

"Yes, Stupid Bastard, I know."

"Fuck you," said Nick, but he felt strangely relieved. "What are we going to do about the pigeons?"

"The ones inside? Kill them." Takehiko poured Corn Pops into a bowl. "I will see about it in a minute. It will not be too easy—I think they are not real pigeons."

"What are they, then?" Nick lowered his voice.

"I don't know. They do not have proper animal *ki*—it is something else. Something I have not see before."

"Right, so they're … Otherpigeons?"

"What are you whispering about, you teenagers?" Yiannis demanded, skipping over to the table.

"Here. Corn Pops." Takehiko presented him with the bowl. "I am going to go see about the pigeons."

Nick followed him back to the hall, which was now looking like Trafalgar Square indoors. Tacky must have talked the apartment into leaving the door of Yiannis's room open. Pigeons were flapping and waddling out of it, landing and taking off in the hall, eddying like bits of garbage in the wind.

Takehiko squared his shoulders slightly, in a little, casual movement, and became that other version of himself that Nick had only seen once before, two months ago. He tore down the hall, raking claw marks of blue fire after him, and pigeons burst in puffs of grey powder on all sides. In a moment every pigeon head in the hallway was turned towards Takehiko. A kind of whirring like machinery vibrated in the air. There was a swish of foul wings, and they were diving from all angles, at one goal.

"*Takehiko!*" Nick screamed. Really screamed.

That only drew the pigeons' attention to him. He found himself suddenly staring down dozens of mad bird faces, blood-red eyes boring into him, bills open in that un-pigeonlike whirring—

He fell back into the blue fire that caught him as gently as water. He might have lain there for a long time, just feeling safe, but Takehiko came bolting back down the hall, snatched him up one-handed as easily as he had picked up Yiannis, and slammed back through the door into the kitchen.

"You are all right?"

Takehiko was leaning over him. The blue fire was gone, but Tacky's eyes were still yellow. His voice came out slightly different around his fangs.

"Yeah, I'm fine." Nick pushed himself up onto his elbows. "You saved my ass. What else is new?" He hoped that didn't sound like sour grapes, because for once he didn't mean it to. "Did you like my anime-girl screaming thing back there? That was pretty nice, wasn't it?"

Takehiko smiled. It wasn't much of a smile—he looked really tired, all of a sudden—but Nick realized he had hardly ever seen any kind of smile on Takehiko's face. Maybe a few times when he had been talking with Rose, but other than that …

"Oh! Dionysus! What happened to you?"

Yiannis was turned around in his chair, staring at Takehiko with horror. At first Nick thought it was because he had not seen Takehiko's other form before; then he realized it was more than that. Takehiko had been holding the front of his yukata closed, but now his hand had dropped to his lap. There was a sort of black crater in his chest. It looked as if something had tried to blast its way through him, and half succeeded. There was no blood, just a big, burnt hole, and something white showing that might have been a piece of his ribs.

"Oh, God!"

"It's … okay. It's not so bad as it looks." Takehiko tried to draw a breath, and then tried to keep from convulsing too obviously with pain.

How can that possibly not be as bad as it looks? Nick wondered. Except that it looked like it would have been instantly fatal, and Tacky was obviously still alive.

"They were … spitting something." He was holding himself up by bracing his hands against his knees, and his face had gone a kind of pale grey. "I … let my guard down, and—one of them got me."

So this part *is* my fault, Nick thought. Throwing-up sounds were coming from Yiannis's direction. Nick didn't blame him.

"Okay." He put his hands on Takehiko's shoulders. "So tell me what a kick-ass yokai needs to recover from being attacked by venomous pigeons, and I'm on it."

Again he smiled. Nick was beginning to think that might be a bad sign.

"I have no idea. Usually … I just sleep." His hands slipped on his knees so that Nick was suddenly supporting him. "Sorry." He righted himself with an effort. "Usually when I have got hurt I just sleep and I wake up better. Yiannis is being sick—could you look after him, please?"

Nick got up without a word. He got a glass of water for Yiannis, cleaned up the mess on the floor and the table, and patted Yiannis on the back and said, "No way!" with great conviction when the satyr whimpered, "Is Tacky going to die?" Actually, he was not at all certain about this; and it didn't seem a very good moment to ask, "By the way, are you immortal, or what?"

When Yiannis was calmed down somewhat, Nick filled another glass with water and took it over to Takehiko, who was sitting with his back against the wall by the hall door, eyes half closed.

"I don't know if this is going to be remotely helpful, but here."

"Thank you." He took the glass of water in both hands, claws clicking on the glass, and sipped it carefully.

"Any chance you can still do that blue flame business?"

"It's … not flames, it's *ki* … "

"Dude—whatever. Do you think you can hook me up with some of it?"

"Like that?"

A thin layer of blue flame—or *ki*, or whatever—danced over Nick's skin, as gentle as water.

"Yeah. Perfect." He got up, flickering blue all over. "Yiannis, can you get the door for me in a sec?"

"What are you doing?" Takehiko asked weakly.

Nick pulled off his T-shirt. "I'm going to take care of the pigeons, so you can get to your room and sleep."

"Nick … "

Yiannis scampered to the door, divided between excitement and terror. Nick knelt and unbuttoned his jeans. He had never done this so deliberately in front of other people before. He had changed in front of those Stake people, but that had been automatically, without thinking.

There wasn't really time for thinking now, either. He couldn't waste Takehiko's power while he sat around dithering. He changed form, wriggling out of his jeans and boxers at the same time. He was getting good at that.

Yiannis held the door open, and the wolf plunged through it. He snapped his jaws on one pigeon neck after another. They were so thick on the ground, it was the easiest hunting he had ever done, although he didn't like the way they disintegrated as he killed them, and the grey powder they turned into made him sneeze. They spat something black and tarry at him from open beaks, but it fizzled out on his lovely new coat of blue flame. They sizzled and puffed into grey powder when they touched him, too. They tried to avoid him by staying in flight, flapping frantically up and down the hallway, but the wolf could jump surprisingly high, and the ceiling of the hallway was low. He picked them out of the air one at a time, until there was nothing left but spatters of grey powder on the walls. Then he went and scratched at the kitchen door until Yiannis opened it again.

The blue flame flickered out and faded as the wolf came back into the kitchen. Yiannis stared past him into the hallway and exclaimed over the lack of pigeons. The wolf was limping badly now; he had almost forgotten his injured paw in the excitement of catching pigeons, but after all that jumping it was hurting fiercely. He limped over to Takehiko.

The wolf knew that this was Takehiko, the friend of that stupid boy, but really he had no category for the thing that Takehiko was. He was not human at all, but he was not an animal either. Right now, the wolf could tell, he was very tired. His breathing was shallow, and the pupils of his yellow eyes had widened from their usual slits. He reached out a hand and buried his fingers in the wolf's fur, his claws scratching gently behind the wolf's ear.

"*Okami-kun ... yokatta desu.*"

The wolf quite liked being petted, but he realized there were more important things to attend to. He nuzzled his friend's hand briefly, then limped off to Nick's room to change.

Changing from wolf to human was always more difficult than the other way around. This was mostly because the wolf never understood precisely what it was that he was trying to do. He had to get the scent of that human boy ...

there it was, in the knot of bedclothes on the floor … then he followed it, carefully, and somehow it led him back to the boy's body. He settled down inside of it, and Nick got up from the floor.

His mouth tasted like pencil lead. He wiped his hand over his lips, and a smear of dull silver-grey came away. He grabbed up some clothes at random and got dressed.

"Hey, Nick, Nick!" Yiannis scampered after him in the hall. "The pigeons didn't shit on my stuff after all! But it stinks in my room now! Nick, how did you get them to go *pouf* like that? That was super cool!"

"I don't know, Yiannis. They just did that." He knelt down by Takehiko again. "I got rid of all the pigeons that were in here. Your blue *ki* stuff really works—they couldn't touch me."

"Mm." Takehiko opened his eyes. "I am quite powerful actually. It is embarrassing that I get … spit on by a pigeon."

"Well, I won't tell anyone. Here—do you want me to help you get to your room?"

"Yes, please."

He didn't really need that much help. Nick kept an arm around his shoulders just in case, but he was able to walk down the hall quite steadily on his own. He knew which room was his, too, so they didn't have to try multiple doors. When they got inside, he leaned back against the door while Nick spread out his futon.

"I can't believe you actually fold this up and put it away every morning," said Nick. "If it were me … Well, you've seen my room."

He went to the window. The sight of the pigeons flapping against the pane and shoving each other off of the ledge just made him tired.

"I'll close the blind, I guess," he said.

"Oh," said Takehiko faintly. "Right."

The pigeons were gone, and it was night outside the window, but the night was lit with neon signs and flashing billboards, and swarming with people. After a moment of startled staring, Nick let the blind fall down over the strange scene. When he turned around, Takehiko was under the covers, apparently fast asleep.

"Hi, is this Nick?"

"Yeah."

"It's John from the Office of Other Affairs. I just got your message. Sorry about that—I guess you called a couple of hours ago. I've been out of range."

"No, that's cool—thanks for calling back."

"So—what's up?"

"Well, Rose is away, and we've got a problem."

"Okay. Well—as your case worker, it's my job to deal with that sort of thing. So what kind of problem are we talking about here?"

"The house is being besieged by pigeons, and Takehiko's been badly hurt."

There was a pause on the other end. "Pigeons?"

"Yeah. Not real pigeons—some kind of pigeon-shaped things that spit venom."

"Uh-huh. And how did this happen?"

"We're not really sure. Some pigeons got into the cakes that I was delivering last night—"

"Oh, Nick—you shouldn't have let that happen!"

"I do my deliveries on a bicycle, sir. I pretty much have to leave it outside. I don't think there was anything I could have done. Anyway, some of them followed me home, and when I got up this morning the whole house was surrounded."

"I see. What does it look like from the outside?"

"What … Well, I have no idea, sir. I can't get out to look."

"You can't get outside?"

"No, sir. There are pigeons all around the house."

"Okay … when you say 'all around the house', what do you mean, exactly?"

"Well, it's like … one of those houses that's attached to the house next door, so I guess technically they might only be on three sides, but they're at the windows that aren't even on the outside of the house."

"They're inside the house?"

"Not now—I mean, you know how the apartment isn't actually in the same space as the upper floor of the house? So some of the windows appear on the inside but not on the outside—but there are pigeons there too."

"Okay. So how many pigeons are we talking about here?"

"Uh … I have no idea. A lot. When you look out any window in the whole house, all you see is pigeons. I've been downstairs to the bakery, and it's the same down there. They're kind of bumping against the glass like they want to get in."

"You've got wards up, am I right?"

"Yes … but not against pigeons."

"Right, but I thought you said these things weren't really pigeons."

"I mean we don't have wards against whatever these things are. It's just the actual windows and doors that are keeping them out right now."

"Uh-huh. How do you know that?"

"Some of them got in. There was an open window, and some others pecked through a screen."

"Wait, I thought you said they weren't inside the house."

"I said they're not in the house *now*. I got rid of them."

"Okay, good. You got them back outside?"

"No, sir. I killed them."

"Uh-huh. What did you use?"

"My teeth?"

"What?"

"I'm a werewolf."

"Right, right. But your wards are still active, is that correct?"

"Yeah, as far as I know. I looked at them, but … my roommate is the one who usually handles that stuff."

"Right. Takahashi. Is he there?"

"Takehiko. Yes, of course he's here, but like I said—"

"Can I talk to him?"

"No. He's asleep. He got hurt."

"Okay, Nick. I have to go—I'm at the ROM and we've got a situation in Ancient Egypt that has to be dealt with. Now I know Rose has got a fairly strong *Innocuous* ward on your place, right?"

"Honestly? I have no clue. That sounds like something out of *Harry Potter*."

"Well, that is the technical term. So what I think you need to do, when your roommate wakes up, is get him to check that and make sure it's at full strength, and with any luck that *should* keep things looking normal on the outside. So if you get any birds inside, you can deal with them, right?"

"Not without endangering my life. Kind of a lot."

There was a long silence on the other end.

"Okay. So you focus on keeping them out. Right?"

Nick sighed.

"Bye, John."

He hung up the phone and went back to what he had

been doing, which was putting a plate heaped with day-old cinnamon buns into the microwave. He zapped them for a minute, and they came out warm and smelling freshly baked. He took the plate down the hall and looked for Tacky's room.

It was quite dark inside, and it took his eyes a moment to adjust to the light of the Japanese billboards that flickered against the blind. He stared hard at the still figure on the floor, until he was sure he saw the slight rise and fall of breathing. Takehiko lay on his back, his hands curled on either side of his uncomfortable-looking Japanese pillow. Nick couldn't quite bring himself to pull down the cover to see whether the hole in his chest was healing or not. He set the plate of cinnamon buns on the floor next to the futon, beside the tray of bread that was already there. The scent curled through the room, and Takehiko shifted slightly in his sleep.

Nick went to the window and peeked around the blind at the nightlife. It would be eleven o'clock in Japan now; he had looked that up online, after reading the Wikipedia article on yokai, which didn't say whether they were immortal or not. The street outside was still crowded with people. But as Nick looked, something seemed to ripple the whole scene, like a reflection in disturbed water. It happened again, and something pointy appeared in the centre of the window and clunked against the glass. In a moment, the night scene had torn open wide enough to admit a pigeon head, red eyes glaring through the glass at Nick. He let the blind drop.

"Shit."

He dashed out of the room and down the hall, frantically opening doors until he found Yiannis's room. The window was shut; the pigeons that had torn their way through the Greek countryside were reduced to pecking and flapping against the glass. Nick leaned in the doorway, his heart hammering so hard it felt like it was trying to get out of his chest.

It wasn't just the pigeons. He hadn't realized how much his ability to cope during the past two months had been due to Takehiko. It was dumb, but he hadn't noticed that the only reason he felt safe at all was because he knew Tacky could take on anyone, and Tacky always knew where he was. There were people in the city who knew that he was a werewolf, and thought that meant that killing him would be good fun. He knew that, but he hadn't been hiding indoors, in fear of his life, because Takehiko could handle it. Not that he had exactly thought about it in those terms. But now Takehiko was out of commission, possibly permanently, and he was rapidly losing his cool.

The living room door opened, and Yiannis poked his horned head out.

"Nick, I'm hungry!"

"Hey, Yiannis. I guess it's about lunch time." He wasn't remotely hungry himself.

"It's ten o'clock," said Yiannis. "But I'm hungry. I threw up my breakfast."

"Yeah, I remember. Okay, um … how about a peanut butter sandwich?"

"All right." He emerged from behind the door, a doll under each arm.

"What do you want in it? Honey, or jam?"

"Banana! Duh."

"Right."

He could do this, Nick thought, chopping banana and slathering peanut butter on bread. He could handle things. He had been doing all right so far. He presented Yiannis with the finished sandwich, feeling like a model of competence.

"You didn't make it the way Tacky makes it."

"It's a peanut butter sandwich, Yiannis. How can Takehiko make it any different than that?"

"He *cuts it up.*"

Nick took the plate away, and cut the sandwich into quarters.

"Better?"

Yiannis shook his head disgustedly. "That's not the way Tacky cuts it up."

"Eat it."

A faint jingling sounded from the entryway, and Nick dove for his school bag and extracted his cell phone. *Please let it be Rose*, he thought. It was a number he didn't recognize.

"Hello?"

"Hey, Nick! It's me."

"Sorry—who?"

"Ryan!"

"Oh, Ryan. Hi. What's up?"

Ryan launched into a long, disjointed story involving TV shows, fighting with his parents, and getting free pizza because the delivery guy had been late. Nick tried to listen, wondering what he was going to say when Ryan asked, "What's up with you?" He needn't have worried, because Ryan never did ask.

"So anyway, the real reason why I called is because we were thinking of gaming again this afternoon. Ranjeet's parents are out of town, and he says we can totally come over. If we start early, you can come, right? I mean, you don't have your cake-delivering gig until when? Eleven o'clock?"

"Ten, usually, but—"

"Cool. We were thinking maybe four or five, so we can get a good couple of hours in before Ranjeet's sister gets home from work. She's probably going to kick us out anyway, because—"

"Sorry, Ryan—I don't think I can make it. Something's come up."

He could have explained to Ryan that he was under siege by venom-spitting pigeons, he thought. But Ryan would have asked what game that was in, and whether he had tried looking up the walkthrough on the Internet.

Then it hit him.

"Listen, man—I'm sorry. I've got to go."

He jabbed END, threw the phone at his bag, and ran to the hall, where he found his room, for once, on the first try, and began pulling *Shadow Legions* manuals off the bookshelf.

Three hours later, Nick was sitting at the kitchen table with every piece of *Shadow Legions* material he possessed spread out around him. Yiannis was under the table again, reading aloud from a picture book called *My First Bacchanal*. The kitchen door opened and Tacky walked in, wholly human-looking again in jeans and a white T-shirt with a large number 21 and a random silhouette of a snake on it. He was licking his fingers.

"You're awake!" Nick leapt to his feet so suddenly that he knocked his chair backwards onto the floor.

"Yay! Tacky's back!" Yiannis scrambled out from under the table and launched himself at Tacky, who deftly warded off his horns while still allowing himself to be hugged.

"Did you put all of those buns and things in my room, Nick?"

"Yeah, I thought the smell might help you recover—you know, amplify your powers or whatever, like it did when you were trapped in the painting." He picked up the chair and set it back on its feet. "I don't know—it was the only thing I could think of."

"It was a good idea," Tacky said. "I think it helped."

"Really? You're all better?"

He looked at Takehiko. He was maybe a little pale, but the white T-shirt fit tightly enough that Nick thought he would have been able to see the black hole made by the pigeon venom through it, if it had still been there. And apparently it wasn't. *Okay, now you can stop staring at his chest.*

"Did more pigeons get in while I was asleep?" Tacky asked.

"Uh, well … "

"In your room, right? I saw this grey stuff on the walls."

"No," said Yiannis, looking up with wide eyes from where he was still clinging around Tacky's waist. "There weren't any more pigeons. I shut my window!"

"Yeah," said Nick. "It was a good thing you did. They pecked through the screen in my room, and a few of them got in. It wasn't a big deal—I killed them."

Tacky gave him a look of raw disbelief. Yiannis looked like he was going to start crying again.

"Okay—maybe 'wasn't a big deal' was an exa—was a lie—but I got rid of them, and I didn't get killed, all right?"

"You could not close the door and wait for me to wake up?" Takehiko demanded.

"No—well, yeah, but I didn't think of that. I didn't know whether you were *going* to wake up."

Takehiko looked at him unfathomably for a moment, then he nodded. "I am sorry to make you worry."

"Whatever. I wasn't—" He realized in time that he was about to say he hadn't been worried that Takehiko might die, which wasn't true and would have sounded awful. "I mean, it's not a big deal. We're all okay, so … "

"He is right," said Takehiko, gently detaching Yiannis from around his waist. "We are all okay. What were you doing while I was asleep?"

"I watched TV for a while, and Nick made me a peanut butter and banana sandwich, but he *cut it up wrong*. And then he was doing something Important and he wouldn't play with me, so I read my book."

Takehiko looked up at Nick.

"I've figured out what these things are. The pigeons. They're a Loft."

"Yes?"

"It's a monster from Shadow Legions, which is a game that—"

Tacky was nodding. "I remember. The game that you play with your friends from school. It has werewolves but they are … un-re-listic."

"Yeah, that's right. The vampires are okay, but the werewolves are really lame. They're just kind of hairy guys with teeth who lose their shit when there's a full moon—they don't even properly change form, and … Anyway, I finally remembered the Loft from SL, and so I looked them up—I've got the GM manual and the *Book of Beasts* because Luís gave me all his gaming stuff when he got married—and that's totally what we've got outside. Look." He found the relevant paragraph in the *Book of Beasts*, and flipped the book around to face Takehiko, then remembered that Tacky couldn't read English and hastily flipped it back. "*In appearance it resembles a flock of pigeons, but the Loft is something much more sinister—a being with many bodies but a single will* … blah blah … It's classified as 'Large Multiform' and it's got a maximum difficulty level of eighteen, which is huge.

It says they whirr, and spit venom that inflicts, uh … level eight burns, which means you'd have to have like level ten regeneration to survive a direct hit—which, um, obviously you do. But the thing is, the reason why there are so many of them is that they self-replicate. They're all one monster, really. There's one pigeon, like the master pigeon, that controls the whole Loft, and just keeps making copies of itself, and until you kill it, you can't defeat the Loft."

"So we have to find the master pigeon."

"Yeah. The Loft Leader."

"How do we tell? It does not glow green, I guess, or have a flashing arrow on top?"

"No. Apparently it's hard to tell. It takes a Perception roll—eight or above on a d12. Then you're supposed to observe that one of the pigeons is producing copies of itself."

"And does the beast book tell you how to kill it?"

"Sort of. It's supposed to be vulnerable only to certain magical attacks. Physical attacks can take out individual pigeons, but not the Loft Leader. He's supposed to be weak against Arcane Magic, but strong against Wood Magic and Wood Magic Users."

"Mm. That is why they could get to the windows."

"Not wood magic as in *magic wood*, stupid. It means like fairies and shit that live in the woods."

Tacky gave him a look. "It is the same thing, Stupid. Where do you think wood comes from?"

"Okay, you have a point. Anyway, the Loft is minus five against werewolves, apparently, so we're in luck there, at least."

"Wait. If the werewolves in this game are not … what you said—not very good—why should we believe what it says about this pigeon thing?"

"Because … I think the pigeon thing was just made up

for the game. I googled *Loft pigeons venom* and all I got were Shadow Legions sites. I don't think it's a real Other that they just used in the game. I think the people who wrote the game invented it. I know that doesn't make any sense ... "

Tacky shrugged. "A lot of the things humans do don't make any sense."

"The only thing I can think of is that somebody genetically engineered them, or, I don't know, conjured them up, or something, to be like the ones in the game. I don't know *why* anybody would do that, but ... they're definitely real, and they're definitely like the Shadow Legions monster, so I pretty much think that's what they are. Anyway, it's all we have to go on."

"Maybe it is a new kind of game," said Tacky. "With real pigeons."

"It's not a game—you nearly got killed."

"That does not mean it is not a game. What is more important is—how do we win?"

"Well, how's your blue *ki* stuff doing?"

Takehiko curled his fingers, making small flames dance in his palm.

"It is okay."

"Do you think it's enough to give me cover?"

"Of course."

"Because one of the things it says here is that if you kill enough of the Loft drones, you can get the Leader angry, and it'll come out and face you."

"Don't do *that*!" cried Yiannis.

"I think we kind of have to," said Nick. "Because we can't go out—we've got to provoke the Loft Leader into coming in here."

"You'll be killed!" Yiannis protested.

"No, we—" Nick started.

"It will be difficult," said Takehiko. "We will need your help."

"Huh?" said Yiannis.

Nick almost echoed him, then thought better of it. "Oh, yeah," he said, "we will."

"What … do you want me to do?"

"Surveirance," said Tacky. "Go to the other windows in the apartment, and look out and see if you can see the pigeon that is lepercating—that is making copies of itself. Then watch it carefully, and find out everything you can."

"And come back and tell you, right?"

"Yes, but knock on the door before you come into the kitchen," said Nick. "That's really important."

"Okay!"

"You mean, 'Roger that!' Right?"

"Yeah. Roger that!"

Yiannis skipped off into the hall.

"It was the best I could think of," said Tacky. "I will tell the door not to open, in case he forgets to knock." He started for the door, but stopped before he reached it. "Bread! Is there any bread in the kitchen?"

"Yeah, there's some whole wheat—"

"Get rid of it!"

"Oh, shit—right. The last thing we need is to have them power up on Rose's baking again. Good thinking."

They tossed the loaf of whole wheat bread into the hall, and between them ate the remainder of a chocolate cake that was also in the kitchen. Nick washed the counter, and Tacky threw the bag of garbage into the hall and gave the door its instructions.

"So," said Nick, "I figured what we could do is sort of like in *Seven Samurai*, you know where they let the robbers into the village one at a time—I mean, not *one pigeon* at a time, but just like open the door for a couple seconds, shut it, kill all the drones that got in, open it again? Does that make sense?"

Takehiko considered for a moment. "Yes."

"Okay, you want to give me a bit of privacy this time?"

"What?"

"I have to change—can you at least look the other way?"

"Why? It is interesting to watch."

"I don't care! Turn around."

Tacky shrugged and turned to face one of the pigeon-filled windows. After a moment the wolf slunk around to look up at him. Takehiko looked down with his yellow eyes, and the wolf gave a pleased skip sideways as the coat of blue fire sprang up all over him again.

Takehiko stretched out a hand, and the door leading to the outside world popped open. The pigeons were so thick outside that it took them only a moment to bump the door open all the way. They poured in, whirring and cooing, to fill the kitchen. The wolf was stunned for a moment by the masses of prey. He hesitated, ears laid back, growling.

The door was not closing. Takehiko spat out something angry-sounding in his own language. He fought his way through the mass of beating wings, clawing pigeons out of the way, to get to the door, and he leaned on it, hard. Pigeons caught between the door and the frame burst in grey puffs as the door finally snapped shut.

The wolf snapped and batted at pigeons. There were so many that he could barely turn around. He was favouring his injured paw more and more now, as it began to pain him again. Takehiko had climbed onto the table and launched himself from there to take down pigeons near the ceiling. He bounced off walls and cupboards, dragging his claws through the pigeons in the air. When a jet of venom came at him, he would spin out of the way, or somersault, or meet it with a fistful of blue fire.

Are you hurt?

The wolf looked around, confused, and realized they had killed all the pigeons. The kitchen was spattered with grey dust and speckled with burnt patches where venom had landed.

Are you hurt?

Takehiko was crouched on the table, looking down at him.

No ... that is old. From before.

The wolf was not used to speaking and being spoken to. The first time Takehiko had spoken to him like that, without human words, it had frightened him. That had been the time before, when he got hurt. When he was hunted. But everything about that time frightened the wolf.

Takehiko sat down on the table, resting his elbows on his knees. He looked down disgustedly at his spattered T-shirt.

"I think we should try something else. That did not work too well. We cannot get rid of them all that way."

The wolf looked up at him and gave a nervous bark.

Can you change back into Nick, please? I am sorry to trouble you. I need you to read part of the book for me.

The wolf wagged his tail, understanding just what he was being asked to do. Why couldn't humans be so clear and polite about things? He limped over to the heap of clothes that the boy Nick had left on the other side of the kitchen, and sniffed for the scent.

"Ow ow ow! Fuck. Don't turn around!"

"Stop sounding like you are dying or something, then."

Nick grumbled and cursed through the laborious process of getting dressed with only one hand, then stalked back around the table to where he had left the Shadow Legions books.

"You're sitting on the Beast Book. Move your ass."

Takehiko hopped down from the table.

"You are really all right?" he asked, looking sceptically at Nick.

"No, I'm not. Changing back and forth all the time gives me a headache, and my hand hurts like fuck."

"Like what?"

"A lot. What did you want me to read?"

"About the Arctic Magic."

"Arcane Magic?"

"Yes. You said it was supposed to be good against the pigeons. I think we should try it."

"Yeah, okay."

Nick tried to brush pigeon-powder off the GM manual, but it just smeared from the cover onto his hand. He flipped through, looking for the magic section.

"The trouble is, you're not really an Arcane Magic User. They're all like, drawing pentagrams and muttering spells and stuff. You don't do any of that—you're more like … "

"Fairies and shit that live in the woods."

"Uh … Yeah. Kind of."

"No, exactly."

"Right. I guess I knew that."

I guess I *should* have known that, he thought. Somebody who could talk to animals—it made sense.

"That is why I am not good at killing pigeons," Tacky added.

"You're doing all right," said Nick. "I don't think any of the Arcane Magic is going to work, though. I think we'd be better off seeing if you can do one of the really high-level

Wood Magic spells." He flipped to the section. "What about *Summon Whirlwind*?"

"Does it tell you how?"

"Um … *roll 1d6 to determine strength of whirlwind* … No. It doesn't really tell you how."

"What else is there?"

"*Cast Thunderbolt, Celestial Hail, Blinding Snowstorm* … "

"Something that is not weather? I am a yokai, not a god."

"All the really good ones seem to be weather. Wait—here's one you can probably do. *Ethereal Fire Chain*."

"I told you it is not fire."

"It looks like fire. That's probably good enough."

"Okay. What do you do? And don't tell me how many dices I am supposed to roll."

"You send out a blast of eerie, otherworldly fire from your hands, and it encircles your enemies and paralyzes them."

"Mm. I'll try. You do the door this time."

"I, um—I can't do that thing that you do." He waved his hand towards the door. "It doesn't listen to me."

"I know that. Just *open* the door. And close it again quickly—don't let in as many as we did before."

"I can't *open* the door if I don't have hands."

"You do have hands."

"I mean—"

There was a bursting noise, and a glassy tinkling from one of the windows behind them. Nick and Tacky looked at one another.

"Oh, shit."

Tacky's *ki* hit Nick this time like a stinging spray, as Tacky himself sprang toward the pigeons pouring through the broken window. *It's a defensive thing really*, Nick thought.

It's not meant to be used as a weapon. Still, Takehiko was doing a pretty good job of making it work.

Nick hauled his T-shirt off again. He was starting to feel like a stripper or something. Through the cloud of beating wings he could just see Takehiko bracing himself and shooting out blue fire from both palms. It frizzled pigeons on contact, but it didn't seem to be forming a ring or paralyzing them.

Pigeons wheeled around Nick, and he stood there dumbly. The wolf was gone. He couldn't change. It was like trying to start a car that had no engine in it. There was just nothing.

Takehiko sprang backwards up onto the table, drew back a handful of blue fire, and drove it forward, ferociously, shouting at the same time: "*Eserear Fire Chain!*"

The fire dispersed in the same way it had before, frying pigeons in its path, but not forming any kind of chain. Nick laughed out loud.

"It was worth a try," said Tacky, shaking back his hair.

"It was *awesome.*"

Tacky looked at him, batting at a pigeon that got in the way. "Why are you standing there with no shirt on?"

"I, uh—I was trying to change, but—" He ducked out of the way of a diving drone. "I don't know what it is—"

Tacky waved a hand dismissively. "Forget it. Look in the book and find me something else to try. Esereum Fire Chain sucks."

"Roger that."

Nick grabbed the GM manual and the *Book of Beasts* and ducked under the table, where it was easier to read without pigeons flapping in his face. Tacky went back to clawing Loft drones out of the air.

"Hey—here's something good!" Nick called. "Wood

101

Magic Users can charge up weapons, because of their ele-
mental affinity, and then—"

"*What*?"

"Weapons! Do we have weapons?"

"I have that katana."

"Brilliant!"

"But I don't think it is sharp."

"I don't think it matters! I'll go get it!"

Nick crawled out from under the table. Over the noise
of the pigeons he heard Yiannis pounding on the kitchen
door.

"Yiannis—hang on a—"

"I saw the boss pigeon!" Yiannis called from the other
side of the door.

"Awesome—um, can you do us another big favour?"

"What?"

"You know that sword that Tacky has in his room?"

"Yeah! You want me to get it?"

"Could you?"

"Just a sec!"

There was a sound of scampering hooves and doors
opening and shutting as Yiannis looked for Tacky's room.
Then he knocked on the kitchen door again.

"Found it!"

"Tell him to come in!" Takehiko called from across the
kitchen.

"Are you sure?"

"If they broke the window here, it is not safe in the rest
of the rooms either."

"Can you protect both of us, though?" Nick asked worriedly.

Takehiko gave him a haughty look, and caught a jet of

venom with a neat burst of blue flame over his shoulder. "You mean all three of us. Yes."

Nick opened the door. Yiannis stood there, wide-eyed, clutching the sheathed katana and flickering blue all over. He shoved the sword into Nick's hands.

"I saw the boss pigeon," he repeated, ducking as a pigeon swooped overhead.

"Yeah?"

"It's really gross. It's this big, fat pigeon, and it goes *hurk hurk*, and pukes up other pigeons out of its mouth."

"Where is it?" Tacky asked.

"It was outside the living room window, but it flew off. I think it saw me."

"Okay." Two pigeons dove at Tacky in unison, spewing venom. He clouted them out of the air in a puff of grey. "Yian-chan, can you get under the table? Nick too. It is easier to protect you if you stay in one place."

Yiannis scampered obediently to the table and slid under. Nick dodged a pigeon that was aiming for his head, and tossed the sword to Takehiko, who caught it.

"How come you've got no shirt on, Nick?" Yiannis asked, as Nick crawled under the table after him. "It doesn't really look very sexy."

"Shut up."

"How come you've got to hide under the table, anyway? I thought you were—*rrrrh*—you know, Mr. Fierce Werewolf."

"You're a brat, Yiannis, did you know that?"

A sheet of flickering blue had fallen down around the edge of the table, like a tablecloth, replacing the *ki* that had been enveloping each of them. Through it they could see Takehiko unsheathe the sword in a cool, practiced way, and give it an experimental swing. The blade gleamed with a deeper blue than everything else they could see.

"Tacky is a lot cooler than you," Yiannis remarked.

"I know that," said Nick glumly.

Takehiko swung the sword, and the blue blade cut through the cloud of pigeons as if they had been made of light. Grey powder poured down.

Nick whistled. "*That* is the way to kill pigeons."

"Yeah," said Yiannis. "With a sword."

Some time in his five hundred years—some time when he hadn't been inside a painting—Takehiko had learned to use a sword. Or at least to fake it pretty well. He sliced pigeons with a clean efficiency, leaving lines of flickering blue in the air as the sword blade passed. The Loft drones were beginning to avoid him, trying to flap back out the window into the throng of beaks and wings pushing their way in.

"Is it a magic sword or what?" Yiannis asked.

"No. He bought it on eBay Japan or something. I don't even know why."

"To defend us from pigeons," said Yiannis. "Duh."

A horrible thought made Nick crawl around under the table to look out at the closed door in the corner of the kitchen. Sure enough, there was a black, burnt patch in the middle of the door, and it was growing.

"Tacky!" he shouted. "Look out! They're coming up from the bakery!"

Takehiko turned with the momentum of his swing. There was a crumpling noise as the door gave way, and something dove through with a *whump, whump* of large wings. Yiannis screamed.

The Loft Leader was a pigeon the size of a pterodactyl— or so it seemed in the confines of the 7C kitchen. Its eyes glowed like red LEDs, its feathers were clumped and greasy, its swollen pink feet ended in vicious claws. A smell like garbage trucks on a hot day rolled off of it. It had been in the bakery. It opened its beak and roared. It sounded like a subway train and a dinosaur and nails on a chalkboard all at once. Under the table, Nick and Yiannis clamped their hands over their ears, and Yiannis whimpered. Tacky stood his ground and yelled back, eyes flashing yellow, lips drawn back from his fangs. The pigeon dove in huge, lurching arcs through the kitchen, convulsing and vomiting out offspring as it went. Takehiko cut down the small, puked-up birds easily.

"Coward!" he shouted at the giant pigeon. "Face me yourself! If you dare!"

From under the table Nick could see the Loft Leader land clumsily on the stove, knocking the spice rack off the wall with a crash. It turned its big head in Tacky's direction, but there was nothing in its eyes to suggest it had actually understood his challenge. The horrible pink feet clenched on the edge of the stove, and the monster took to the air again with a flap of its huge wings. There was a hissing, spitting noise, and something flared yellow. Yiannis squeaked. Nick shoved a chair frantically out of the way to peer out from under another part of the table. The Loft Leader was breathing fire.

Tacky had caught the jet of reeking, smoky flame against his sword, one palm against the back of the blade. The pigeon's fire spattered and fizzled against the blade, but it was clearly all Takehiko could do to hold it off. He snarled in frustration. There was a ringing sound as the sword blade cracked.

The wolf leapt out from under the table and launched himself at the bird. His paws hit its back, his teeth sunk into its neck. He bore it to the ground. Its magic jittered along his bones, but he held on, bit down harder, snapped the thing's neck with a wrench of his head. He backed off, panting and trembling. The thing was not dead, but Takehiko had reached them now, and he drove the broken-off sword into the bird's body. It fell in on itself strangely, pattering down onto the linoleum in grey powder that formed a lopsided picture of what it had been. The small pigeons that still filled the room and surrounded the house melted like mist.

For a moment it was quite silent in the kitchen. Then Yiannis scuttled out from under the table to stare at the remains of the boss pigeon, and Takehiko dropped to his knees beside the wolf and hugged him. The wolf licked his face, even though he had a funny feeling that he shouldn't do that. There was something else that bothered him ... or not *him*, exactly, but that boy. He bounded off down the hallway.

"It was a drawing!" Nick said as he burst back into the kitchen. "That's what the whole thing was to start with—it was a drawing of the Loft Leader from Shadow Legions!"

"You've got your T-shirt on backwards," Yiannis informed him.

Takehiko had taken his own T-shirt off altogether, and was leaning against the fridge, looking down at the picture on the floor with a grim expression.

"It was a pencil drawing," Nick went on. "That's what this stuff is—pencil lead."

"Yes, I figured that out, Nick."

"Oh. Well—I'll tell you what you didn't figure out. It was from Ryan's sketchbook—I had it in my school bag, and I left it outside next to the cakes when I went into that place with ... when I did this one delivery. That's how it got brought to life, I bet. From the smell of the cake. Like ... " He stopped.

Takehiko looked at him. "Yes," he said. "Like me. Only,

if you were wondering, I was a real demon before I was a painting. That thing was a drawing before it was anything else."

"Oh," said Nick. For a moment he *had* wondered.

"I will tell you what I would like to know. Where did your friend get the pencil that he drew this with?"

"He's not … Okay, he is my friend. I think I know where he got the pencil from. I mean, I think I know *who* he got the pencil from. Does it matter, do you think?"

Tacky raised his eyebrows. "You think it is just his great artist skill that made it come to life?"

Nick looked down at the pigeon on the floor. It was an okay drawing—it was definitely better than anything he could do—but he could see Tacky's point. It must have something to do with the pencil. Maybe it was coincidence that only one of Ryan's drawings had come alive. Or maybe it was because that was the only one in the sketchbook that had been drawn with Laura's pencil.

"There's a big hole in this door," Yiannis remarked in the silence.

"Yes," said Takehiko, "there is."

"Oh, shit. Guys—the pigeons were in the bakery. You know what that's going to mean?"

It was late evening when Rose got in. She burst through the back door of the bakery and stood there, the worried look on her face giving way to confusion. She looked from one boy to another, then at the mops and buckets of soapy water, then back at Tacky.

"You're all right? There was a message from Nick on my answering machine when I got home, saying that something had happened to you. But—but you're all right. I mean—are you?"

Takehiko smiled up at her from where he had been kneeling to scrub the floor. "Yes, I am fine. We are cleaning your kitchen. There were some pigeons." He looked across at Nick. "You called Rose."

"Yeah. You were half dead. Of course I called Rose."

"I—I know that I say you guys don't have to tell me things," said Rose, "but—I think this time I might make an exception."

After a moment of glancing at one another they began to talk at once.

"It was—"

"There was this—"

"—Nick's fault, because—"

"—and Tacky was totally—"

Rose held up her hands. "Actually, you know what, it can wait for tomorrow. So long as you're *absolutely sure* everybody is all right … "

"Yes," they all said together.

"Then I'm going to let you get back to cleaning my kitchen, because … Did you say there were *pigeons*?"

"They were a monster really," Yiannis supplied.

"Yeah. Um … I see you found the bleach. That's good. Carry on. Yiannis, why don't you come upstairs with me? I have some good news for you."

"Really? What is it, what is it?"

"Come up to the apartment and I'll tell you about it. Let's leave the big boys to finish their work."

"They're going upstairs," Nick observed, as the door shut behind Rose and Yiannis.

"Yes."

"She's going to see the state of the apartment."

Tacky shrugged. "We were going to tell her anyway. At least we got this clean."

"I wonder what she has to tell Yiannis. Hey, do you think she's found a family for him?"

"Maybe."

"I hope so. It must suck for him to be stuck here with us. I mean, if that place outside his window is where he's really from. It looked pretty sweet."

Tacky nodded.

"What was the place outside your window, anyway? I mean, I figured it was Japan, but ... "

"It is called Harajuku. It is a ... place with stores, in Tokyo."

"A shopping district?"

"Mm."

"That's kind of weird."

"Not really. Five hundred years ago it was a forest."

"Oh. That was where you lived?"

"Yes."

"Do you ... " *I can't believe I've never asked him this before*, Nick thought. "Do you ever get homesick?"

"Home ... sick. No. I am not human, Nick. That place is not my home. It is my parent, and my child, and part of myself. And it doesn't know me any more."

And it wasn't even the right question.

Tacky got up and dried his wet hands on his jeans. "Those were details. Rose would not approve."

"No, it's cool. I mean—I'm sorry."

"That place upstairs does know me, a little bit. It is crazy, but it does know me. It does not show me Harajuku out my window any more, unless I tell it."

Nick got to his feet too. He couldn't think of anything sensible to say. He had been living with Takehiko for half a year, and he hadn't *thought* that he understood him very well. But the funny thing was, Tacky seemed a lot more human to him just then than he usually did.

"I don't know about you," Nick said, "but I'm hungry."

"I am starving."

"Yeah, killing demonic pigeons really takes it out of you, eh? Plus cleaning. I don't know which is worse, actually. There's food upstairs, but … I'm guessing you don't feel like cooking."

"Good guess."

"Me neither. What do you feel like having?"

"Something with meat."

"Me too. Mother's Dumplings is open late—maybe I could go get some takeout."

Takehiko looked at the door leading up to the apartment. Nick thought of the chaos of the kitchen above them. The rest of the apartment was not much better.

"Is it far?" Tacky asked.

"No—just on the other side of Spadina." He had no idea whether it mattered or not, but he added: "And it's late, so … it probably won't be busy."

Tacky nodded. "Why don't we go out?"

"All right! *Swift death to dumplings!*" Nick held up a hand.

Takehiko smacked it. For an instant he was grinning.

They headed for the door.

BIRDS OF A FEATHER

(BONUS PAGES)

THE STEREO ON TOP of the fridge was blasting a compilation of '80s music that Nick's brother Carlos had made for him. It was Yiannis's favourite. He was capering around the newly clean kitchen, singing along to some ridiculous synthesizer song. It was a definite improvement, Nick thought, over the sobbing and screaming which had been his first reaction to Rose's news. Tacky was sorting laundry in the corner by the washing machine. Nick was sitting at the table, trying to fill out a form.

"Yiannis," he said, seizing his opportunity as the song ended, "how do you spell your last name?"

Yiannis stopped skipping briefly, and leaned on the back of a chair to chant out: "K-E-R-A-S-T-O-P-O-U-L-O-P-O-L-O-U-P-L-O-"

"Yiannis! I'm filling this out in pen—will you be serious?"

"K-E-R-A-S-T-O-P-O-U-L-O-S."

"Okay ... Birthplace?"

"Mount Parnasos National Park."

"Mother's species."

"*We're birds—doot-doo,*" Yiannis sang along with the stereo, "*of a feather—doot-doo!*"

"Yiannis, can you calm down for two seconds?"

"I'm going to AUSTRALIA!"

Yiannis pushed himself off from the chair and skidded towards the washing machine. Tacky straightened up hastily and caught him by the horns.

"Pay attention to Nick," he said, walking Yiannis around so that he was facing the table. "You have to fill out the form *before* you can go to Australia."

"Oh, okay." Yiannis climbed obediently into a chair and sat waggling his hooves and only mouthing the words to the song.

"Right," said Nick. "What species was your mother? A. Nymph or B. Human?"

"Nymph."

"Cool. Um ... 'Previous place of residence' is here, obviously ... 'What special talents do you bring to Syrinx Colony?' Let's just put 'Enthusiasm' and ... 'Energy.' You've already been accepted, right, so it probably doesn't matter what we put."

"*And baby, we're gonna fly ...*"

"'Name of Primary Sponsor,'" Nick read out. "White, Rose. 'Relationship.' Um ... Landlady? I don't know. I'll leave that blank and she can fill it in. 'Species.' Human. 'If human, secondary non-human sponsor must be specified.'"

"Put down Tacky." Yiannis twisted around in his chair. "You're going to be my non-human sponsor, right, Tacky?"

"What do I have to do?"

"Nothing—you just have to have your name on the form. Do you know how to spell Tacky's name, Nick?"

"Yeah—we've been through that one before. I'm always having to fill out forms for him. H-A-Y-A-S-H-I—T-A-K-E-H-I-K-O. 'Relationship.' L-A-Z-Y—A-S-S-H- Oh, sorry, that's 'Job Description.'"

"Tacky's not a lazy asshole!"

Nick wrote down *Friend*.

"What?" said Takehiko belatedly.

"'Species.' Do I put 'demon', or what?"

"Mighty. You put Mighty Demon."

Japanese demon, Nick wrote.

"*We're birds of a feather*," went the song. "*We're in this together.*" Doot-doo, doot-doo, doot-doo …

Nick flipped to the next page of the form. "'Check all that apply: A. Horns.' Check. 'B. Horse ears.' No. 'C. Hooves.' Check. 'D. Tail.' Check. 'If checked, please specify: A. Long or B. Short.' I'd say your tail is short, right, Yiannis? Let's go with B. Okay … 'What is your … *favourite kind of nymph*?' What? 'A. Naiads. B. Oreads. C. Leimoniads. D. Dryads.' What the heck is a 'leimoniad'?"

"It's a meadow nymph," said Yiannis. "But dryads are my favourite. My mommy was a dryad."

"Okay, cool. Dryads. D. 'How much wine can you drink before passing out?' Uh … 'G. Unknown.' Next question. 'Do you prefer … ' *What*? I can't believe they're asking that! 'NOT APPLICABLE.' What the fuck?"

"What was it?"

"I'm not reading it out. It's totally not applicable. You're *eight*."

"Nick," said Takehiko, "what are these?"

Nick looked up. Tacky had a pair of Nick's jeans in one hand, and several small green plastic packets in the other.

"Uh ... "

"They were in your pocket. Are they important?"

"They're condoms!" Yiannis sang out delightedly.

"Oh, those," said Nick. *Fucking satyr.*

Tacky looked at the things in his hand as if he had just been told that they were slugs. He deposited them on top of the dryer and wiped his hand on his jeans.

"How come you've got your pockets full of condoms, Nick?" asked Yiannis.

"Yiannis ... " said Takehiko. "I do not think we need to know." He went back to putting clothes into the washing machine.

"I thought you didn't even have a girlfriend, Nick!" Yiannis persisted.

"I don't. It's not like I'm planning on using those things. Some smart-ass Sidhe gave them to me as a joke. I didn't even remember they were in my pocket."

"Mm-hm," said Yiannis. "Sure. What's your girlfriend's name?"

"I don't have a girlfriend! God. I'd have told you guys before now if I did."

"Yian-chan, shame on you."

"Huh?"

Tacky turned around, leaning on the dryer. "Why does it have to be a girlfriend? Maybe he has a what-do-you-call—a man friend?"

"*What*? No way!"

Yiannis squealed. "Do you think?"

"No, not really. I just wanted to see that look on his face." He was grinning as he turned back to the washing machine.

"You guys are both bastards," said Nick.

He looked back down at the form. He was going to miss

Yiannis, he realized. So was Tacky—probably more, since the satyr had been his only constant company in 7C.

"I would totally tell you if I had a girlfriend," Nick repeated. "I mean, not that it's *ever* going to come up, but—I'd probably even tell you if I had a boyfriend."

"You'll have to message me in Australia to tell me," said Yiannis, a little sadly.

"Oh, I will. I mean really, from the sound of this place where you're going … I'm probably going to be messaging you to ask for advice."

7C GOES DOWN

THE DEER HAD ONLY been herself for a few minutes, but she knew what to do. Her hooves hit the wet grass in a frantic pattern, her legs gathered themselves under her and flew out, every muscle strained with the imperative of flight. Behind her, low and silent and gaining, ran death.

He was lean and silver; his eyes gleamed yellow-green in the weak light. When she swerved, he matched her movement. When she stumbled on the uneven ground, he gained further.

She tore out from among the trees and made a leap for the top of the wet, wooden structure that loomed in front of her. She landed awkwardly, her hooves booming on the hollow surface. She scrabbled to right herself.

The wood was slippery, and the wooden thing plunged away behind her in a smooth curve. She was sliding down it, backwards, her legs buckling under her, too frightened to regain control. She came to rest at the bottom, tried to heave herself up, and he was upon her.

Her legs thrashed, and she twisted her neck away, but she could feel his breath on her hide. Then, only for a moment, she felt his teeth.

12 hours earlier

"It's okay," said Brianna, fishing her house key out of her backpack. "There won't be anyone home but us."

She darted a glance at the elf as she jiggled the key in the lock. He was managing to stand more or less upright, but his face had gone incredibly white. It kind of suited him. It made his cheekbones stand out, or something, and his eyes seem brilliantly blue. What a terrible thing to notice, Brianna thought. She was amazed at herself.

She got the door open and stood clutching her backpack awkwardly while he dragged himself inside. He leaned against the kitchen counter near the sink, and slid down until he was sitting on the floor. He pulled out the hand that had been clutched inside his leather vest. It glistened with blood. Brianna must have made some noise of horror, because he smiled reassuringly up at her. It obviously cost him some effort, but his smile was breathtaking.

"Pray forgive my rudeness," he said, resting his wrist on his knee and cradling his hand to keep from dripping blood on the floor. She noticed again his musical accent. "My name is Cian. May I know yours?"

"Brianna Baker." She caught herself about to add, "Pleased to meet you," like an idiot.

He smiled again. "May I beg you for a cup of water, Brianna Baker?"

"Oh! Yeah. Just a sec."

She dropped her backpack, grabbed a mug from the draining rack, and stuck it under the faucet. When she knelt beside him with the full mug, he put his clean hand on hers to guide it to his lips. *This is really happening*, she thought. The touch of his hand made it seem more real.

"Are you … " She swallowed hard. "Are you really badly hurt?"

"It is a trifle merely. A scratch. Yet I fear I must beg your assistance in one further matter."

"Of course! What do you need me to do?"

His pale hair parted in soft strands around the sharp, unmistakable point of his ear. That was real. And what had happened by the dumpsters in the parking lot, that had been real too.

"Help me to assess … the extent of the damage. If you would be so kind … "

"Okay." This meant taking off some of his clothes; she had figured that much out.

He wore a green tunic under the leather vest, laced together at the neck, and leggings of a darker green, and tall, pale leather boots. Brianna took hold of the edge of the vest, and tried to ease it over his shoulder without moving him. It was embarrassingly difficult. In the end, he had to lean forward from the cupboard so that she could get his arm out of the vest, and then she reached awkwardly around behind him for the other arm, before he suggested, in the kindest possible tone, that she might want to get it from the other side.

"Oh—yeah. Right."

What had happened in the parking lot had been too fast

to follow, especially while telling herself that it wasn't really happening, but he had evidently been hurt on his right side. His tunic was torn there, and soaked with blood. She thought she could make out toothmarks, and she was surprised not to feel sick.

"That thing that attacked you ... " she began.

"The *cu sith*," he supplied. "A fairy hound. It answers only to its mistress."

"The ... um, the elven queen?" She looked up into his eyes, and reeled a little. They were just so blue.

He nodded. "My lady."

"Wait ... *your* lady? But you're, like, a—a good elf or whatever, right? I mean, your queen's not *evil*. Is she?"

"No, indeed. She is not evil. But she can be slow to forgive, where she feels herself slighted. Pay it no mind, Brianna Baker. These are matters that need not trouble a mortal maiden."

Nobody had ever referred to Brianna as a "maiden" before. For a moment she felt a horrible desire to giggle. She concentrated fiercely on the tunic. She got it unlaced, and pulling it over his head turned out not to be nearly as awkward as getting the vest off. His skin underneath reminded her of the inside of a shell, but he had impressive muscles for somebody so pretty. There *were* teeth-marks, and blood running down in little rivulets. Still, this wasn't as awful as Brianna had expected. She remembered the scene in *Lotus Song* where Mariko bandages Chang Wei's arm after reading about how he was injured in the Book of Unfolding, and the thought bubble said something like: "This is so much worse in real life!" Only this was real life, and oddly, it *wasn't* so much worse. And Cian was much prettier than Chang Wei. Brianna wadded up a dishtowel and thrust it into his hand.

"For—to—you know, stop the bleeding. I'll get you a wet one, too."

He had become unexpectedly awkward, and she had to hold the dishtowel against his bare side for him. He rested his hand on her shoulder. She began to worry that he was going to faint, and then, if she wasn't careful, maybe hit his head on something. On the other hand, if he sort of collapsed sideways into her lap, she thought, that wouldn't be so bad … In fact, it might be kind of nice.

He murmured something which she couldn't catch.

"What?" she said.

He looked up into her eyes. "My dusky princess," he murmured.

"*What*?" She was pretty sure he meant that to be nice, but it sounded kind of racist.

He looked perplexed. "What is the matter? Does it trouble you to hear me praise your beauty? Human girls of any colour have held but little interest for me, I confess."

"Oh." She still wasn't sure about that, but for a moment, as she looked into his blue eyes, it made her feel special.

And then he did faint, collapsing sideways just as she had imagined, to lie across her lap. His pale hair was spread across her knees, and one hand flopped on the green linoleum of the kitchen floor. The bite in his side couldn't have been very deep, because it had almost stopped bleeding. Or maybe elf blood clotted more quickly … She wanted to just sit there and look at him. There didn't seem to be anything else she needed to do.

She heard the key turning in the front door, but she went on sitting there, looking at Cian. She heard her mother coming into the hall, dropping her gym bag by the door, and calling out, "Brianna? Are you home?" but she went right on sitting there. Cian stirred a little, and she watched his face, eager to see his eyes open again in their extraordinary blueness.

"God Almighty! Brianna, what are you doing?"

Brianna looked up, startled. Her mother was standing in the kitchen doorway, staring in with horror.

"There was an accident." She felt as if she had just woken up. "He got hurt."

"That's when you call an ambulance, child—haven't you got any sense?" Brianna's mother was looking at Cian now. "Who are you?" she demanded. "You don't look very hurt to me. What sort of 'accident' was it?"

Cian was awake, and sitting up—somehow Brianna had missed noticing when this happened. She felt cheated.

"Dear lady," he began.

"He got bit by a dog," Brianna cut him off. "A *cus* … something—it belongs to the queen of the fairies, Mom, not that you'd understand that. He's a fairy—I mean an elf—I mean … "

"I don't care if he's a vampire or a hobbit, Brianna, if he was bit by a dog he needs to get a rabies shot at the hospital." Her hand was already on the telephone receiver. "I thought you had more sense."

"Dear lady, I beg of you—" Cian began again.

"You don't believe me, do you, Mom?" Brianna cried, jumping to her feet. "I *knew* you wouldn't believe me!"

"Sweetheart, I work in a high school. I know all about role-playing and cosplay—I didn't think you were into all that, but lots of girls your age are."

"It's not something I'm *into*, Mom! Look at him! He's got pointed ears!"

Ms. Baker looked at Cian for a moment. "So he does," she said in a strange voice.

She dialled 911, still looking at Cian. There was a crash,

the kitchen window shattered into fragments in the sink, and something bounded through, snarling.

It was the dog from the parking lot, which Brianna only thought of as a dog because that was what Cian had called it. It was huge and shaggy and green, with a grotesque, snarling mouth. Sparks crackled off its fur, and its tail snapped and hissed with yellow-blue flame. It lunged for Brianna's mother. Brianna screamed. Cian, beside her, had leapt to his feet, but before he could move to distract the dog's attention, the creature had dropped heavily to the kitchen floor. Brianna's mother had torn the telephone off the wall and brought it down on the dog's head, stunning it. In another moment she had seized a knife from the counter and stabbed it cleanly into the creature's shaggy side. The dog twitched once, and blood spread on the linoleum.

This time it was not Brianna who screamed, but the elf Cian.

"What have you done, woman?" he shrieked. "You have killed him! My precious pet, my *cu sith*, you have killed him, and you shall pay! To the death I will fight you! To the death!"

"Do you want me to tell you what you have to do?" Takehiko asked, rearranging himself on the couch so that his head was pillowed on one arm.

Nick sighed. "No. But I don't know what to do. So—what do I have to do?"

Takehiko hauled his hair out from under himself with his free hand. "You have to turn into the wolf, then you can follow the scent."

"Ugh—why didn't I think of that?"

"I don't know."

On the TV screen, the green-hatted figure crouched down and melted into wolf shape. It looked good, Nick thought, but he couldn't say how realistic it was. He'd never seen it happen from the outside, for real. And the game didn't give any idea of how it *felt*, how the wolf came out from inside you, where he had been waiting.

He looked over his shoulder at Tacky. "Are you just going to lie there and watch me, or what?"

"Yes."

"Awesome. Do you want to play Soulcalibur or something instead?"

Tacky gave a one-shouldered shrug. "We could."

Nick drew a deep breath and tamped down his rising annoyance. *If you're not even going to try to cheer up …* But that wasn't how it worked; he knew that. He crawled around behind the steamer-trunk that the television was sitting on, swapped out the plug from the old Nintendo for the one from the Playstation, and found the Playstation controllers behind a display case of stuffed birds. The living room had been in a weird mood all week.

After a few rounds of Soulcalibur, Nick was ready to give up on that tactic. Tacky was usually able to make his wispy girl character break Nick's axe-wielding giant effortlessly over her knee about four times out of five, but today he didn't even seem to be trying.

"You know what? I've got an English essay I should really be writing. You've got stuff to watch, right?"

"Mm. I can turn on the TV."

Nick slid his controller irritably across the floor and got up. "Okay, you do that then."

Outside in the hallway, he stood staring discontentedly at the ceiling. The English essay wasn't due for another three weeks. It was just the first thing that had popped into his mind.

He couldn't stand it, this constant awareness that Takehiko was unhappy. It had been like this ever since Yiannis left. It *would* be depressing, Nick thought, to be stuck in an apartment with only him for company. And the place really was quiet without Yiannis. The satyr had flown to Australia more than a week ago. A woman with wafting blonde hair and a faint smell of pine needles had arrived from Syrinx Colony to chaperone him, and he had gone off to the airport with her, bundled up in boots that made him walk funny and a hat that hid his horns. On the doorstep he had made loud, tearful promises to phone and Skype, but Nick wasn't surprised that they hadn't heard from him yet. He was living in a place where he could go outside and play in the sun with others of his own kind. Calling Nick and Tacky wasn't going to be uppermost in his mind. Meanwhile, 7C had gone back to being as quiet as before Yiannis came to live there. Nick didn't mind that much, himself, although he did miss Yian-chan. But to Takehiko it seemed to make a big difference. Looking after Yiannis had been Tacky's job, and he was clearly bored without it.

It wasn't just Yiannis leaving, either. Ever since the night after the pigeon attack, when Takehiko had explained about his forest, Nick hadn't been able to get that out of his head. To be stuck in a downtown apartment in a big city, when you really belonged in a bamboo grove somewhere on the other side of the world—that would absolutely suck. Somehow, pointless as it was, he couldn't stop thinking about that. And he was getting tired of it.

He went to the kitchen, poured himself a glass of some off-brand cola that he had unwisely bought on sale, and stood leaning against the washing machine, looking around the kitchen while he drank it. The kitchen was spotless. Most of the cleaning was Tacky's job anyway, and these days he was even doing bits of it that weren't. The other day Nick had come home to find that Tacky had actually folded his laundry. He went back down the hall, found the door to his bedroom, and propped it open with a flip-flop.

There was a full-length mirror behind his closet door. He pulled off his shirt and stood in front of it for a minute. He looked into his own eyes, wide open but shadowed in his human face, and something made him decide he didn't want to see this, after all. He turned his back on the mirror.

The wolf nudged the propped-open door with his paw and slunk through. The living room door, which was always the same one, was easy to open; it swung in, and the knob just needed the barest twitch to pop the catch. When the door swung open, the wolf bounded through, forepaws hitting the ground energetically.

Takehiko was still lying on the couch where Nick had left him. He had not even turned off the Playstation; the "Choose Your Character" screen from Soulcalibur was still glowing on the television. He moved the hand that had been resting over his eyes, and looked across at the wolf.

"Do you want to be let out or something?"

The wolf loped across the room and stood beside the couch to look at Takehiko. He looked like a human boy, the wolf thought. And smelled like one, too, when he sniffed him. His eyes were very dark.

The wolf surged up onto the couch and stood on top of Takehiko, his forepaws squarely on the boy's shoulders, his nose in Takehiko's face.

"*Okami-kun*! What's up with you?"

Takehiko looked the wolf in the eye and ran his fingers through the wolf's fur. He was smiling. The wolf, who had thought he was doing this because Nick had wanted him to, found he was pleased in his own right. After all, he and that boy Nick had some things in common. He made a happy attempt to lick Takehiko's face.

Get off, said the boy who was really something else. *You're heavy.* His eyes flared yellow for a moment, and he bared his teeth at the wolf. And the wolf, who had never seen a display of dominance before, nevertheless knew exactly what it was, and not only bounded off the couch but immediately shrank down on the floor, ears laid back, tail tucked between his legs. Takehiko laughed, a wild, dangerous laughter.

The wolf stretched his legs and shook himself, then settled on the floor beside the couch, head between his forepaws, tail flicking nonchalantly. Takehiko lay back down on his side, and after a moment reached over the edge of the couch to pet the wolf. For a long time they remained like that.

The phone ringing disturbed their tranquility. Tacky hoisted himself up and reached over the back of the couch to pluck the phone off a little table cluttered with conch shells and glass paperweights.

"Hello ... Hello, Mrs. Pel-era." He got slightly tangled up in the consonants, and the wolf saw him wince. "He will call you back in one minute, all right? He is not—can't—come to the phone ... Yes!" He laughed, tucking his hair behind his ear. "That is what I mean, yes. But, I am Japanese, so ... Yes! You understand ... Thank you. I will talk to you later. Goodbye."

He hung up the phone and slid back down to sit on the couch, elbows on his knees, and looked at the wolf.

"You heard. Your mother. I said you would call back."

The wolf stared up at him, obstinately uncomprehending. He didn't have a mother. Takehiko frowned.

It is time to be Nick again, he said. That, reluctantly, the wolf did understand.

Takehiko was in the kitchen when Nick came back out of his room. He had put on some anime theme music and was washing rice in the sink.

"What were you and my mom giggling about back there?" Nick asked.

"Oh, just because I said that you could not come to the phone, and she said, he is in the bathroom, right? She thought it was funny that I am too polite to say that. I like your mother. She always wants to have a conversation."

"Yeah, that's true. Sometimes it's good—sometimes it's not." He turned down the volume on Tacky's music, picked up the kitchen phone, and dialled his parents' number.

One thing, Nick thought, he was grateful for, although he was never going to mention it, because not having to talk about it was kind of the point. Tacky had never shown any inclination to ask that question that started, *Aren't you ever going to tell your mother …* Nick didn't know the answer to that question.

His brother Tony answered the phone, and launched into a long, rambling story which Nick was pretty sure was going to end with a request to borrow money. He was right.

"No, man, I've got no money, and I'm pretty sure that's a pyramid scheme or something. Can you put Mom on the phone, please? I know she's there because she just called me."

While he waited for Tony to get an answer to his shouts of, "Mom! Nick's on the phone!" the lights went off in the kitchen.

"What's that?" he asked, looking at Tacky.

"I don't know. I just plugged in the rice cooker."

"You must have blown a fuse. You can't have that and the stereo plugged in at the same time, or—Hi, Mom. What's up?"

His mother had a message from his grandmother, who wanted someone to run an errand for her. This often happened since Nick had moved downtown, because he was now the closest grandson to hand. He didn't mind.

"I have to go out," he said to Tacky. "You know how to fix the fuse, right? It happened before, and we fixed it, remember?"

"Yes," said Takehiko. "I remember."

He looked a little doubtful, but Nick decided to ignore that, and left for his grandmother's house.

"So what actually happened?" Denise Baker sat on the living room floor in her dressing gown, a mug of hot tea in her hands, in front of Brianna, who was curled up on the couch. "Honey? I'm mixed up in this now, so you'd better tell me the whole story."

"It sounds so dumb," said Brianna.

"Well, these things do, when you just say them. That's normal."

"What do you mean, *these things*?"

"Oh, you know—traumatic things. It doesn't matter what kind of supernatural stuff might be going on, it's still just plain old trauma, at the bottom of it. It's like anything else."

Brianna didn't know whether she found that comforting or depressing.

"First of all, when did you meet that guy?" Denise asked, looking searchingly at her daughter.

"In the parking lot behind the high-rise towers," said Brianna.

"When?"

"This afternoon—just before you saw us. Just a few minutes before that."

"Are you sure?"

"Yes!"

"You never saw him before that in your life?"

"Never in my life!" Brianna hauled herself up into a sitting position on the couch. "Look, I'll tell you what happened. I was coming home through the parking lot of the apartments, and it was around the back near the dumpsters. I was in a hurry because I'd just bought the new volume of *Different Hearts*, and I wanted to get home and read it. And I saw that *thing* come out from behind one of the dumpsters, with flames coming out of its tail, like you saw, and Cian jumped down—I don't know where he jumped from, but it almost looked like one of the apartment balconies, because he landed on top of the dumpster, on the lid, cause it was closed. And he jumped down from there, and the dog thing turned around and saw him, and it attacked him. It bit him on the shoulder, or … well, that's what I thought at the time, but actually it was on his side, sort of—and it got him down on the ground, and he shouted out. I don't know if he was calling for help or not, but that's what I thought. I mean, I thought I should help him. I sort of … I had my backpack, and I sort of ran at the dog, swinging it. I know that was stupid, and I could have got hurt, I *know* that … "

"Brave, stupid—same difference," said Denise, sipping her tea.

"Anyway, that's all, really. The dog ran away—I don't know if it was scared of me, or … that's what I thought, anyway."

"Probably he had it trained to do that. But what did he do then?"

"Well, he was lying there bleeding. I wasn't going to just leave him."

"Honey, I'm not going to tell you you should have just left him. You should have called the ambulance, but—"

"I *know* I should have called the ambulance! I don't know why I didn't. I had my cell and everything. I just … I looked at him, and he was looking back at me, and I sort of got all muddled." She felt incredibly stupid thinking about it now. "All I could think of was how cute he looked. I can't *believe* that was what I was thinking—and I sort of remember thinking that, too, like 'How can I be thinking this at a time like this?' Also I saw he had pointy ears. And then he said … 'Will you do me a kindness?' or something like that, and I felt like, if he'd asked *anything* I'd have done it. That's when he told me he was from the, um, fairy court, and that he needed me to hide him somewhere, and some stuff about how I was the only one who could help him." She was ashamed to think she had really believed this. "I said he could come home with me, because there was no one here. That's all—then I helped him up, and we got back here, and I was helping him wash off the blood and things. But I still felt like all I could think of was how cute he was, and how I just wanted to sit there and look at him. I didn't even think of calling an ambulance."

"What did he look like to you?" Denise asked.

"What do you mean?"

"I mean that I think he looked different to you than he did to me, sweetie. You said he looked cute."

"Yeah … I mean I know he's like white or whatever, and I said I didn't like white boys, but he was just so … with his long hair, all silvery-blond like that, and his eyes were so *blue.* I don't know, I can't describe it. Just really, really cute. But that's no excuse, anyway! I don't get insane just because I see some cute boy!"

"No, but I think it probably is an excuse. You thought he looked how old? Your age?"

"A little bit older—maybe like Grade 12."

"Right. Because to me he looked middle-aged. Kind of wrinkled around the eyes. His head too big for his body, you know, with wrinkled little hands. *Ugly.*"

"What?"

"I think he really was a fairy, Brianna, or an elf, or what-ever you want to call it. I think that's why he looked different to you—he was putting his glamour on you, making himself irresistible to you, so you couldn't do anything but think about how pretty he was. That's what they're sup-posed to do. I remember reading about it when I was a little girl. My babysitter gave me a book about fairies."

"Did he ... did he look to you like he had pointed ears?"

"Oh yes. I could see them clearly, on account of his re-ceding hairline."

Brianna winced.

"Mom, what are we going to do?"

"Well, I think I'm going to have to fight this Cian—if that is his real name." Denise got to her feet and tightened the knot of her dressing gown belt. "If I know how these things work at all, I don't think I'm going to have any choice. I'll call Sandra and ask her about this business of being my sec-ond, and I'd better look up what time dawn is tomorrow. And then I think we had better get a good night's sleep, both of us."

Early morning bread delivery was Nick's favourite part of his job at Heaven and Earth. Since the episode of the pigeons, Rose had been encouraging him to take her car instead of his bicycle, and sometimes he did that, but he still preferred the experience of cycling around the quiet city before dawn. And the deliveries were quicker on the bicycle, because he couldn't take Rose's car onto the Paths (the Sidhe would admit a bicycle, but balked at the amount of metal involved in a Honda Fit).

The advantage of the car, though, was that it could carry a lot more than the bicycle, and that morning, when Nick put his head in the bakery door and saw the size of the pile of bread to be delivered, he decided he had better take the car. He didn't mind; driving through the deserted streets was fun, too. He ran back upstairs to get the keys and return his bicycle helmet to its home on the floor of the hall closet. He flicked the light switch in the kitchen to no effect; the fuse had not been replaced. Tacky wasn't up yet, so Nick left without berating him. He thought to mention it to Rose, but she was busy in the bakery kitchen when he came down. He loaded fragrant, fresh loaves of bread into the back seat of the Honda and drove off.

It was an easy morning; there were several large deliveries that took care of most of the bread, and none at too great a distance. The morning air was sharp with cold, and he did not regret being inside the deliciously bread-scented car. It had rained in the night, and the moisture was still in the air, and glimmering in puddles on the roads. One customer was a no-show, although Nick followed the elaborate instructions about turning three times, standing on one foot, and knocking on the door left-handed with his eyes closed. This left him, gratifyingly, with an unclaimed bag of cinnamon buns to tear into as he drove back downtown.

His last stop was in a park close to Heaven and Earth, a delivery that he had overlooked on his way out. By now the sky was pale pink overhead. He parked the car on Bathurst and set off through the park, the last bag of bread in one hand, a cinnamon bun in the other. There was something going on in the empty swimming pool behind the community centre, he noticed as he passed by. He found the bench where he was instructed to leave the bread, left it, and started back to the car. Out of curiosity, though, he made a detour by the swimming pool, eating the last of his cinnamon bun as he went.

He stopped behind a row of trees that screened one end of the pool. He wasn't sure, now, how he had been aware that something was going on here. It was pretty effectively hidden from sight. But when he stopped to look, it was alarming.

There were five people in the bottom of the dry swimming pool. Three were standing on the sidelines, watching: a woman, a teenaged girl, and a Sidhe man with wings and a long grey cloak. The other two were fighting.

They were unmatched in every way. The Sidhe combatant, a wizened, ugly little figure, had a long, glittering rapier that drew arcs and eddies of green in the air as it moved. It was a horrible, sickly green that reminded Nick of the colour of an approaching thunderstorm. His opponent was a tall black woman in a purple track suit, armed with a wooden kendo sword. But she was holding her own. As Nick watched, she swiped aside the green rapier and hammered the ugly little Sidhe into a retreat. She even caught him a sound blow across the ribs with the wooden sword.

"She's winning!" Brianna exclaimed with fierce delight.

"Shh," said Ms. Gianelli, casting a wary look at the other fairy man standing stone-still beside them: Cian's second. "Don't get too excited. Of course she's winning—she coaches the girl's *and* the boy's kendo teams. But I still don't understand why she's fighting this little man with his toy light sabre. It's not like your mother."

Brianna said nothing. Ms. Gianelli was doing the thing that she had fully expected her mother to do: stubbornly interpreting everything in terms of a perfectly natural explanation. Denise knew that it was not a toy light sabre. Goodness knows what it was—but it was pretty clear you couldn't win against it with a bokken, no matter now many kendo teams you coached. Cian had kept repeating, "To the death!" just to make it absolutely clear that Denise would have to kill him if she wanted this to be well and truly over.

Cian—if that was his real name—looked to her now exactly as her mother had described him. When they had arrived at the swimming pool for the duel, he had still seemed to Brianna like the beautiful boy from yesterday afternoon, but as he fought with her mother, he seemed to grow older, wrinkled, his hairline crawling back from his forehead, his eyes turning from bright blue to glittering, insect black. He couldn't keep up the glamour while he was concentrating on the duel. Surely that was a good sign.

The green sword darted towards Brianna's mother, and its owner gave a horrible, toothy snarl. Denise managed to dodge, but only just. It wasn't going to be enough, Brianna thought despairingly. How could she possibly kill someone like that?

Something up above, on the brim of the pool, caught

Brianna's attention. She looked up, taking her eyes off the duel for just an instant. Someone had stepped out from behind the trees at the end of the pool, and he was looking down on the duel. It was a white boy, the age that she had thought the fairy was. He was blond, but in a more realistic way, with streaks of brown. His face was pale, but his eyes did not glow amazingly blue. He was an ordinary boy. Except that he wasn't, because somehow, after a moment, behind him or *through* him she could see that he was really something else altogether: something green-eyed and snarling, something that could have grabbed the *cu sith* in its jaws and snapped its neck in one shake.

"Hey!" He was just a boy again, shouting. But he *was* shouting. "Hey! You can't do this shit in a public park!"

Nick didn't know quite what his plan was when he shouted at the duellists. It was the desperate look in the girl's eyes that made him do it. He felt he had to do something. She looked like she was maybe in Grade 9, and she was obviously about to lose her mother to some fairy bullshit, if someone didn't do something.

The combatants paused tensely. The fairy in the cloak drew a sword of his own, and spread his filmy insect wings.

"Anyone who would stop this duel must deal with me!" he announced, in a fruity voice.

"Yeah?" said Nick, slipping his cell phone out of his pocket. "Because I think I'm just going to call the police and let them deal with you."

Several things then happened very quickly. The fairy duellist lunged, and the tip of his rapier struck the girl's mother in the shoulder. Sickly thunderstorm green flared up and down her arm, and she convulsed with pain. The girl screamed. The fairy rounded on her, raising a hand in a savage gesture, and the girl seemed to melt, horribly, and then harden into a new, inhuman shape. Her hooves skittered on the painted concrete of the swimming pool. Nick had only had time to turn on his phone and punch 9.

The mother spared only a moment to stare in horror at what had happened to her daughter. She flew at her opponent, and her wooden sword clunked against his skull. He crumpled to the ground, his rapier spinning out of his hand. She seized it and plunged it into his chest.

The deer bolted up the sloping shallow end of the pool and scrambled out. She was off into the park in a moment, running hard. She would go out into the street and get hit by a car, Nick thought, or get lost in the city. He took off after her, peeling off his jacket as he ran.

The wolf could run faster than that boy. He flew after the deer, gaining steadily on her as she dodged uncertainly among the trees of the park. He was on his home turf; he knew this park well. He was doing something that he had never done before, but that felt like part of his nature. Something he knew he was good at. This was what wolves did.

He was very close now. The scent of the deer was intoxicating. She ran into the skatepark, leaping for the top of the wooden half-pipe. She landed awkwardly, her hind legs slipping off the platform. He arrived at the bottom of the curve and waited, panting, for her to slide down.

Maybe it was those moments of waiting that released him from the chase and let him realize what he had to do. He could see, as she slid down the half-pipe, that she was still a girl, wrapped round with an enchantment in the shape of a deer. She probably thought she was a deer, but she was really still a girl. Perhaps it wasn't that he could see this; perhaps he could smell it. He knew it, at any rate. He heard running feet in the distance, and shouting, but he ignored them.

He leapt at her when she reached the bottom, pinning her down, and sank his teeth into the illusion of the deer. Bitter-tasting green magic spilled out. He tore back a strip of the enchantment, peeling it away from the girl underneath, and spat it into the grass. The deer form buckled and wobbled as the girl struggled back to herself, pushing her way out of it. Finally the empty deerskin flopped away and disappeared, and the girl sat shivering at the bottom of the half-pipe, with acid green rivulets running off of her clothes and her hair.

The wolf looked up. The woman who had been fighting the fairy, and the one who had been standing on the sidelines, and the other fairy, the one with wings, were all coming through the trees. The two women wore looks of horror. That was what the shouting had been about. They had seen him set on the deer who was really a girl, and sink his teeth into her throat. They thought he had intended to kill her. The wolf stood aside, swishing his tail diffidently and holding his head high, letting them see that the girl was fine, he hadn't done anything to her.

The two women reached the girl, and there was a scene of human emotions from which the wolf turned away. The winged fairy strolled up and nodded to him.

"You must be the delivery boy from Heaven and Earth," he said, flicking his wings with a papery rasping. "Well done there. No hard feelings, I hope. I'm sure we can keep this matter quiet, and it will be better for all parties. My master is dead now, so I believe I'll make myself scarce."

The wolf drew back his lips from his teeth ever so slightly, and the fairy smiled and melted away among the trees.

A trail of crusted, drying green led from the swimming pool to the skatepark. The wolf looked across at the girl's mother, kneeling at the bottom of the half-pipe with her daughter, while the other woman stood over them. She did not seem to be bleeding, but that didn't mean she wasn't hurt. He loped off in the direction of the swimming pool, scanning the ground for Nick's discarded clothes. This was something that boy could handle better than he.

Nick ran up to the group in the bottom of the half-pipe, his jacket in his hand, untied shoelaces flapping. The woman duellist was in obvious pain. She was holding the shoulder that had been hit by the fairy's sword, and looking at the fingers of that hand, which she held out stiffly and awkwardly. The other woman was kneeling beside her now, looking perplexed and angry. She was one of those people who looks put-together even in a crisis. She had neat brown hair and fancy glasses, and her sneakers were the same shade of orange as her jacket.

"Hi," said Nick awkwardly.

The women and the girl looked up at him.

"Who are you?" demanded the orange-sneaker woman.

"Uh, I'm Nick."

"No, but who *are* you? What do you have to do with all of this?"

"He was the wolf," said the girl, faintly.

"What?" Orange Sneakers demanded. "*What?*"

"Yeah," said Nick. "I'm sorry about that."

Orange Sneakers looked furiously from the girl to Nick, as if she thought there was some sort of conspiracy between them. She, Nick realized, and not the hurt mother or the traumatized daughter, was going to be the hardest to deal with. She was deep in denial.

"I think," said the black woman in a quiet voice, "that I'm turning into wood."

"Oh," said Nick. "What makes you think that?"

"What?" said Orange Sneakers again. Everyone ignored her.

"It feels … " The black woman pulled back the sleeve of her jacket from her injured shoulder. It was light enough now that Nick could see she was right. Above the elbow, her arm had turned a whitish grey, with streaks of black, exactly like birchbark. She was turning into a tree.

"Yeah, that looks … not so good."

"What is it?" the girl asked fearfully. "What's going to happen to her?"

"Hopefully, nothing. I, uh, I've got a car," Nick said, gesturing. "The woman I work for, she knows about this kind of thing—she can probably help you, or if she can't, she'll know who can."

Orange Sneakers got to her feet and gave Nick a stern look. "What is 'this kind of thing'? Who is the woman you work for?"

"Her name is Rose White. You wouldn't know her. I can call her if you want." He dug in his jacket pocket again for his phone. "But we don't really have a lot of time."

"Why don't you start by telling me just exactly what has happened to Denise's arm—and what that green stuff is, anyway."

"I don't know *exactly*. It's some kind of fairy magic, but other than that … " He shrugged.

Orange Sneakers sighed angrily. "What is it really? This is serious, young man."

"Look. Lady. It's *really* fairy magic. Really. You need to stop pretending there's some 'rational explanation.' Your friend's daughter was just turned into a deer. You *saw that*. Fucking deal with it."

Behind Nick, the girl giggled unsteadily.

"Don't you take that tone with me," said Orange Sneakers, just exactly as Nick had expected she would.

"Yeah, whatever."

The girl was pressing her knuckles to her lips and shaking.

"What are *you*?" the mother asked, looking up at Nick.

"Well, I'm a werewolf, but … " He felt this just confused matters and would have preferred not to go into it.

"Great," said Orange Sneakers, nodding with satisfaction. "Great. You're a werewolf. I'm going to call the police, which is what we should have done a long time ago." She produced a Blackberry and began making good her threat.

"I wouldn't do that," said Nick.

She took a step away from him. "Are you threatening me?"

"I am *so* not threatening you. You're the one who's saying you're going to call the police. But I wouldn't do it, because, for one thing, they're not going to be able to do anything for you, and for another thing, the Sidhe—the fairies—okay, the *gang* that you're dealing with, that your friend is mixed up with? They're really good at keeping below the radar. It's very unusual for people to come into contact with them, or any of their, um, *criminal activities*, and be able to spread the story around. I really don't think you want to go calling attention to something like this."

"What would happen?" asked the woman on the ground.

"Mostly this kind of thing, I think." He nodded towards Orange Sneakers. "But they can only get so far with denial and forgetfulness—you'd run the risk of getting disappeared altogether if they realize they can't keep this quiet any other way. I really think you'd be better off coming with me."

"You saved my daughter's life," the woman observed.

"I was in the right place at the right time."

"And did the right thing. I trust you. Sandra, put the phone away—you're not going to call the police. Help Brianna up. Where is this car you said you have?"

Orange Sneakers took charge of the girl, Brianna, which left Nick to help the mother. She seemed all right except for the arm that was turning to wood. But even in the time it took them to get to Rose's car, the infection, or whatever it was, had spread, and she could no longer bend her elbow except in a stiff, creaking sort of way. Nick was glad there were few cars on the road, and the journey back to Heaven and Earth would be quick.

When they reached the car, Orange Sneakers insisted that all three passengers sit in the back seat, with herself and the girl on either side of Denise. What she thought Nick might do that would make it dangerous for one of them to sit in the front with him, he didn't ask.

She kept at him all through the drive, trying to get him to explain what was going on in some way that didn't involve fairies or magic.

"Believe me, young man, I'm not as ignorant as you suppose. I know all about larping."

"Yeah?" said Nick. "Good for you."

"That's what this is, right? A role-playing game?"

"It's not a role-playing game, Sandra," said Denise wearily.

"I was asking him," Orange Sneakers insisted.

"Nope," said Nick. "It's not a game. At least not for us. It might be a big joke to the fairies—well, except that one of them is dead now, so ... they might not be too terribly amused about that."

"Dead? That little blond man? He's not dead!"

Nick cast a worried glance over his shoulder. "No?"

"He's dead," said Denise grimly.

"What?" Orange Sneakers exploded. "Then, then, then we really should have called the police! Denise! Surely!"

"Ms. G.," said Brianna, speaking slowly and apparently with an effort, "please ... please calm down. I don't think ... the police ... needs to know about him. Because he's not human."

In the rearview mirror Nick could see Orange Sneakers looking wildly between Denise and her daughter, obviously trying to decide which of them was the craziest. Then she turned back to Nick.

"Stop the car!"

"We're almost there. I'll stop in just a minute."

"Stop the car!"

"In a minute!"

"STOP THE CAR!"

Nick had turned into Kensington. A delivery truck in front of a fruit stand blocked half the street ahead, and as Orange Sneakers lunged forward to try to wrest the steering wheel from Nick's grasp and drive from the backseat— or whatever it was she was trying to do—the truck began to back up. The car was careening straight for it. The girl screamed. Nick pushed Orange Sneakers away with his elbow and swung the car out of the path of the reversing truck. He pulled into the alley beside Fountain of Youth in a blind fury. In front of Heaven and Earth, he jerked the parking brake savagely and threw open the car door.

"How can you be such an idiot?" he yelled back through the open door at Orange Sneakers. "You nearly got us killed!

I don't care how much denial you're in, there's no excuse for that shit!"

He left the car door open and stalked towards the bakery door. It opened as he approached, and Rose came out. He felt pitifully glad to see her.

"What's going on?" Rose asked, with that air she had of being concerned without wanting to sound like a mother.

"Somebody got in a fight with a fairy in Alexandra Park. She's, uh—it looks like she's turning into wood? Birch, I think. So I thought I'd better bring her back here."

It was such a relief to turn things over to Rose. Nick watched her go out into the alley to the car, pulling off her floury bandanna and stuffing it in a pocket of her apron, and take over the situation in her cheerful, competent, Rose way. He leaned against the doorframe as she introduced herself to Orange Sneakers, sticking out her hand to give that surprisingly firm handshake that she had. "Mm-hm, yes, mm-hmm," she said, smiling away sympathetically, as she gently detached the injured woman from Orange Sneakers, and beckoned to the girl to come out of the car.

"It's *all* going to be *okay*," said Rose, steering the whole party towards the front door of Heaven and Earth.

That was her signature phrase, Nick thought, as he held the door open and got out of the way. She had a certain way of saying it, and you really believed her. He remembered Rose telling him it was *all* going to be *okay* when he first came to Heaven and Earth eight months ago. It was hard to believe it had been such a short time, actually. So much had changed. But the thing was, even at that time, he had believed her. And he hadn't been wrong. She was Rose White, after all.

Inside the bakery, Rose guided Denise into a chair and helped her pull off her jacket. The tree-infection had spread alarmingly. Distracted as he had been by Orange Sneakers' antics, Nick had not noticed, but half of Denise's face was whitish birchbark, and there were small leaves sprouting from her hair.

"Nick," said Rose, not taking her eyes off Denise, "in the kitchen, on the far wall, there's a first-aid kit. Can you bring it to me?"

"Sure."

He ducked into the kitchen and came back with the cookie tin that was kept near the door, with "First Aid Kit" written on it. Rose was getting Orange Sneakers and Brianna to sit down at another table. She took the kit out of his hands with a grateful smile, and laid it on the table beside Denise to open it. Inside were the usual bandages and bottles of rubbing alcohol, and a few other, odder things. She withdrew a dark bottle with a yellowed, typed label that read "Primrose-Caraway Preparation."

"What is that?" Orange Sneakers demanded, starting up from the table where Rose had deposited her.

"Primrose-Caraway—it sounds like a hippie shampoo, doesn't it?" said Rose cheerfully, uncapping the bottle and taking out a wad of gauze from the kit. "But it's actually very effective. When it's a magic weapon you're dealing with, it's best applied to the point of impact." She sloshed the contents of the bottle generously onto the gauze, and handed it to Denise. "Just slip it under the strap of your top, and hold it there, if you can," she said. Denise nodded and did as instructed. "It won't *reverse* the process now, unfortunately, but it will stop it in its tracks."

"Yes," said Denise slowly, after a moment. "I can feel that it's … slower. Yes."

"Great!" said Rose. "Now." She turned to Brianna. "For you. Cinnamon bun or apple turnover?"

"Um … " The girl looked confused.

"What?" Orange Sneakers demanded.

"Oh, you can have one too, of course. I have pecan pie as well, but that's not really part of a complete breakfast, is it? Or, if you prefer, I can just make you some toast."

"I've had breakfast, thank you," said Brianna timidly.

"Not *my* breakfast, you haven't. I'll bring you a cinnamon bun—if you like you can just nibble a bit. I guarantee it will make you feel better. I'll bring you one, too," she added, looking at Orange Sneakers. "Nick, will you give me a hand for a moment?"

He followed her into the kitchen.

"Bad scene!" she said when the door swung shut behind them.

"Is she going to be okay?"

"Yes, I think so. Thanks to you—you're a star! But she was very nearly a tree. I think she was starting to think like a tree. Here." She took down the bakery phone from its cradle on the wall, and handed it to him. "I think I've got the Whitebeam Services number in there. I don't know if it's her new one, though. Give it a try, anyway."

Cristina appeared from the basement with a bag of flour. "What is going on? I hear voices."

"We've got a bit of a situation," said Rose. "Sidhe-related."

"Who-related?"

"Fairies."

"Ohh!" Cristina rolled her eyes. "Fairies! I hate them. We are nearly out of brown sugar."

"Thanks," said Rose, expertly levering sticky cinnamon buns out of a pan and depositing them on plates. "One for you too, Nick?" she asked, looking up at him.

"Sure." He didn't mention that he had eaten a couple already that morning. "I don't need a plate. I'm getting a *this number is no longer in service* message."

"I thought you might. The number for Other Affairs should be in there as well. Could you call them and ask if they have Whitebeam's current contact info? They should. If they don't want to give it to you, pass me the phone and I'll deal with them." She grinned.

Nick dialled the Other Affairs number obediently, taking a bite of his cinnamon bun. They returned to the front of the bakery, where Rose handed around plates with buns. Orange Sneakers pushed hers away disdainfully.

"It looks *terribly* sweet," she said. "For heaven's sake, Brianna, don't eat that whole thing."

Brianna nodded, but she was already taking her second large bite.

Someone answered at the Office of Other Affairs after a few rings, but it was the night security person, who didn't know the answer to Nick's question. He said he would see if anyone else was in yet, and put Nick on hold. Rose was putting more Primrose-Caraway Preparation on another piece of gauze, and explaining that they were trying to get through to someone who would be able to help. The Office of Other Affairs had some very strange music that it played to people on hold. Nick stood leaning against the doorframe, holding the phone a little away from his ear and licking cinnamon stickiness off his fingers.

Brianna was looking up at him and smiling tentatively. She had finished her cinnamon bun and was looking like she was starting to feel better, as the effect of Rose's baking took hold. He smiled back.

"I'm on hold," he said, indicating the phone.

"Oh."

"I'm Nick, by the way."

"Yes, you said. I'm Brianna."

"Right. Sorry about the, um … "

"Oh, but you had to do that, right?"

"It seemed that way, yeah."

"So … you're a werewolf?"

"Yeah."

"Wow."

"Well, it's not like in *Twilight* or anything."

"No?"

"Actually, I don't know—I haven't read the books or seen the movies. I just have a friend who's always going on about how unrealistic it is, and … But she's a vampire, so … "

"Oh."

The night watchman returned to the phone to say that he had checked downstairs without success, and was now going to look upstairs because he thought he had seen a light on there.

"So," said Brianna to Nick, "vampires and werewolves are friends?"

"Friends? Oh, well, Cristina is more like a co-worker. I know a few other vampires, but I don't know any other werewolves. But we're all friendly, yeah. It's mostly with the fairies that you get the weird factions and stuff. They're bad news, for the most part." He laughed. "It's a bit to take in, right? I haven't even been here that long, but I guess I knew about some of the weird shit in the world since I was thirteen."

"I'm fourteen."

"Oh yeah? Well, if you have any questions … "

"Okay. Thanks."

"How did your mother get involved in all this, anyway?"

Brianna sighed anxiously. "It was my fault."

It was really such a relief to explain everything to Nick. He reminded Brianna a little of Eiji in *Peppermint Candy*—something about the way his hair fell in his eyes. Eiji had never been her favourite character, of course; he was just too polite, and never got his own way. But in real life, she could see the benefit of a polite boy. Nick was very polite. He nodded and looked sympathetic all the while she told her story, and in the end she believed him when he said he didn't think it was her fault.

Brianna had only been a deer for perhaps fifteen minutes, but she found that the feeling lingered. Even now she couldn't stop thinking about how it had felt to change form, to feel the body that she was used to suddenly betray her. It had been like the ground giving way beneath her feet, only worse, falling into another shape, another form of existence. In the car on the way to the bakery she had still felt like a deer: frightened and skittish, and like she should be walking on all fours. Things smelled strange, and when she wanted to say something, it took her a moment to remember how to talk. Being inside the car had made her feel horribly penned in and trapped. The only thing that had kept her calm was the boy who had been the wolf. He didn't have to *do* anything; it was just something about the way he was. The way he had talked back to Ms. Gianelli had cheered Brianna up immensely.

"Your mother's super-brave," he said when she got to the part about the duel. He looked impressed.

Now that she was feeling human again, she found herself becoming increasingly aware that she was covered in green ooze. It didn't seem to be doing her any harm, although it was uncomfortable, and bits of it were beginning to dry on her arms and in her hair. But she must have looked awful. She wished she could see a mirror, or, better yet, get into a bathtub.

"There's really weird music playing," Nick said, making a face. "Want to hear?"

"Sure." She held the phone gingerly up to her ear, trying not to get green ooze on it. She heard a faint bonking, clanking noise, and snickered. "Are you sure it's music?"

"Good point. Hey, do you want to get cleaned up? That must be kind of uncomfortable. Your mom's going to be okay," he added when she hesitated. "Rose has got everything under control here. I can show you where the bathroom is upstairs, and you can wash off. Better yet, Cristina can take you."

He leant through the door to the kitchen and called out, "Hey! Cristina, can you do me a favour? Come on, we're not opening any time soon, you can spare a few minutes."

After a moment, a sulky, pale girl about Nick's age emerged in the doorway, wiping her hands on her apron.

"What?"

"Can you take Brianna upstairs and help her find the bathroom, and, like, help her out or whatever? She's got fairy gunk all over her."

Cristina looked Brianna up and down. "Dis*gust*ing," she pronounced. She had a strong foreign accent, and there was something about the way she said dis*gust*ing which made it sound sort of extra-disgusted. "Here. Come." She turned away towards the kitchen.

"Wait, wait!" Ms. Gianelli was scrambling to her feet over by the table where Brianna's mom was. "I'm coming too. I'm not letting you out of my sight, Brianna."

"Fine," said Brianna. "Whatever."

Nick shot her a sympathetic look, then turned his attention to the phone. "Hi, it's Nick Pereira from Heaven and Earth," he said into it. "Yeah, hi. Fine. I mean I'm fine, but we've got a bit of a problem here. Again. Yeah."

Brianna and Ms. Gianelli followed Cristina through the kitchen, which looked pretty much like a normal kitchen of a bakery or a restaurant or whatever, with big mixers and ovens and a glistening row of freshly baked pecan pies lined up on a long table down the middle. Brianna was trying to remember whether Cristina was the name Nick had used when he mentioned the vampire co-worker, and wondering whether she should say anything about it. Was it polite to mention that sort of thing? More to the point, she thought, should she be worried? It was probably just as well that Ms. Gianelli hadn't heard that part of the conversation, although it would just have started her raving about larpers again.

At the back of the kitchen was an open doorway, and beyond it a flight of dark, steep stairs going up. Cristina climbed the stairs, and Brianna and Ms. Gianelli followed. The doorway at the top was filled with one of those curtains made of wooden beads. It clattered as Cristina pushed it aside, and swung back in Brianna's face. "No manners," Ms. Gianelli muttered under her breath, reaching out to gather the beaded strands and hold them out of the way for Brianna.

On the other side of the curtain was a short, dingy hallway, with depressing floral carpet and several metal doors on either side. It reminded Brianna of the inside of the apartment building where her friend Sue lived. Cristina was standing in the middle of the hallway, looking puzzled.

"Well?" said Ms. Gianelli after a moment. "Which one is the bathroom?"

Cristina gave her an angry look, as if this were a totally

unfair question. "How should I know? It's not *normally* like this."

"No?" said Ms. Gianelli. "What's it *normally* like?"

"It's a kitchen," said Cristina, as if this should have been incredibly obvious.

"I see," said Ms. Gianelli. Brianna could tell that she was thinking this Cristina person obviously did drugs. "Well, how about you take a look for the bathroom for us, hmm? It must be behind one of these doors."

"Don't patronify me," Cristina growled. But she stalked to the end of the dingy hallway and pulled open a door. Multi-coloured light poured out from inside, and music. "What?" said Cristina, sounding really puzzled. Then in a moment she had stepped through the door, and it had slammed shut behind her, with a metallic thud.

They waited a few moments, but Cristina did not reappear.

"Well," said Ms. Gianelli crisply, "at least we know *that's* not the bathroom. Come along, Brianna."

She pulled open the nearest door, brisk and businesslike now that she was not faced with obviously supernatural things that she had to pretend were a role-playing game. Brianna longed to say something like, "Yes, let's find the bathroom quickly so that I can wash off this MAGICAL GREEN FAIRY GOO." But she was a little scared of Ms. Gianelli, to tell the truth, and didn't quite dare.

Ms. Gianelli shut the door again quickly, a puzzled expression on her face. Brianna didn't get to see what had been inside, but evidently it wasn't the bathroom either.

"Let's try another, shall we?" said Ms. Gianelli.

"Okay," said Brianna, and without waiting for Ms. Gianelli, turned the handle of the door nearest her.

The door swung in, and was heavy, so that Brianna had to take a step inside the room to open it all the way.

She was in a ballroom. A polished wooden floor stretched away towards a little stage at the end, between rows of tall windows hung with crimson curtains, and chandeliers glittered overhead.

"Wow," said Brianna.

"The bathroom must be down at the end," said Ms. Gianelli. "Look."

There were two doors at the end of the room, on either side of the little stage. Somehow Brianna had a strong feeling that neither of them would be the bathroom they were looking for, but she couldn't quite put it into words. Anyway, she doubted Ms. Gianelli would have listened.

"Okay," she said. She held the door open for Ms. Gianelli, who strode through and marched down the ballroom, her sneakers squeaking loudly on the polished floor. Brianna let the door close quietly behind her and followed.

The room was beautiful, she thought as she walked down between the rows of windows, but there was something about it that bothered her. It was the windows, she realized. She turned to look at one. It was one of those windows that come all the way down to the floor and open like a door, and it looked out onto a vast moonlit garden.

Brianna stood fixed to the spot with cold horror. They were on the second floor of a house in a back alley, and it was early morning. Everything about the view outside the window was wrong.

They must go back down to the bakery. It wasn't really so urgent to find a bathroom. She turned, and saw that they couldn't go back. The far wall of the ballroom was covered in uninterrupted floral wallpaper, with no sign that there had ever been a door in it.

At the other end, beside the little stage, Ms. Gianelli was opening one of the two remaining doors.

"Wait!" Brianna shouted, pelting down the room.

"Calm down, dear," said Ms. Gianelli. "It's not as if we're going to get lost."

"Cian," said Rose thoughtfully. "No, it doesn't ring a bell. But as you say, it's probably a pseudonym. His real name might have been Gimp, or Shady Bob. Fairies often have strangely unpicturesque names."

"I am sure that I killed him," said Denise worriedly. She formed her words with difficulty because half of her face was stiff and wooden.

"Well, it was certainly self-defence," said Rose. "*And* you were defending your daughter."

"But what about ... his people?"

"Oh, they do things like this by the book. They are quite keen on rules and prohibitions and that sort of thing. If it was a duel, he was taking his life into his own hands, and they won't seek revenge. I have seen it before. I don't think you have to worry about that."

"Even the guy's own servant didn't seem to like him much," Nick added. "He definitely wasn't clamouring for revenge—he just kind of took off."

A timer went off in the kitchen.

"That's the gingerbread," said Rose. "I'll be a few minutes. Nick, can you take over? The Primrose-Caraway should be refreshed in another minute or so. I wonder what's become of Cristina?"

"Maybe she's helping them run a bath."

"Maybe," said Rose doubtfully. "Not terribly like her, though."

"It's okay—I can take care of things. Go deal with the gingerbread."

Rose thanked him and disappeared into the kitchen. Nick sat down across the table from Denise. She smiled with the side of her face that wasn't wooden.

"You're very helpful, Nick."

"No problem."

For some reason he found himself thinking of his own mother. Not that she was much like Denise on the surface. Marie Pereira was small and blonde and delicate-looking, and people were always being amazed and a bit alarmed by the number of sons she had. You could tell people wondered just how young she had been when Ed, who was nearly forty, was born. She liked to let them wonder. She never explained that Ed, Tony and Luís were stepsons—not even, on one memorable occasion, to the police. She took it all in stride. She could probably have taken the truth about Nick in stride too. Probably.

As if she could tell what he had been thinking, Denise remarked, "I hope you've got someone at home who's proud of you."

"What? Oh, well, I left home. I guess this is my home. So … I'm good. I've got people."

Denise nodded.

"You're a pretty cool mother, I've got to say," Nick remarked after a moment. "I mean, not just the sword-fighting and everything—that's obviously awesome—but from what Brianna said, it sounds like you didn't make a fuss about, you know, ohmygod fairies, there's no such thing as fairies!"

Denise laughed—or tried to, and winced slightly. "Sweetheart, I am not that awesome. When I saw Brianna in the kitchen with that awful little man, and she tried to tell me he was an elf or something, I thought she was on drugs. Really and truly. If his green dog hadn't jumped through the window the next moment with its tail on fire, there's no way I would have believed any of it. Well, there were the pointed ears—that was a bit strange. But you see, his glamour wasn't working on me. I know why now, too. I just thought of that."

"Yeah?"

"When I was a little girl, my babysitter was obsessed with the fairies. She had this stuff in a little tin, it looked a bit like one of those expensive lip balms, and it smelled of herbs. She told me it was fairy ointment, and if you put it on your eyelids every night before bed, after two weeks you would be immune to the fairies' illusions. I think she must have known what she was talking about."

"Cool," said Nick.

Rose returned from the kitchen. "How are you doing?" she asked Denise.

"I've stopped feeling so much as if I need to stand in the earth somewhere and put down roots. That's a relief."

"Yes, it is that."

"I should get out of your café, though. Won't I frighten your customers?"

Rose laughed. "Not very likely. But you might be more comfortable upstairs—things can get crowded on a Saturday morning. Let me go fetch Cristina to mind the shop, and then we'll take you up."

Nick opened his mouth to offer to go himself, but he had just upended the bottle of Primrose-Caraway Preparation onto a new piece of gauze, and it slopped out over his hand, demanding his attention. By the time he had the situation under control, Rose had gone back through the kitchen, and he could hear her voice calling up the stairs.

"Cristina!" There was no answer. "Cristina! Cristina, don't make me climb these stairs to come look for you!"

"Rose, I'll go!" Nick called out. But Rose must not have heard him, because he could hear her footsteps going up the stairs.

"No, no—if we go back through the gymnasium and take the *left*-hand door, we ought to get back to that room with all the plants, and that will take us to the hallway with the paper lanterns, and we know that's connected to the walk-in fridge, *which is connected to the ballroom*. You see, it's quite simple."

Brianna stared hopelessly at Ms. Gianelli. *Are you even listening to yourself?* she wondered.

"Okay," she said, because it seemed the easiest thing. "Let's do that."

"Now … the gymnasium was through … " Ms. Gianelli turned back from the dining-room table to contemplate a row of doors which had been rearranging themselves subtly even while Brianna watched. "It was this one, I'm quite sure," she said, striding to a door and pulling it open.

Of course it wasn't the gymnasium. The gymnasium, Brianna was sure, was long gone. But Ms. Gianelli just thought she had got the door wrong, and tried another. And another.

"Well, that's very curious," she said, when she had tried them all. "None of them leads to the gymnasium. We must have—oh, I see what must have happened. We've got turned around—we actually came through another room *between* this one and the gymnasium. Now, I wonder which one that was."

"Ohmygod!" Brianna had completely lost patience with this. "What is the *matter* with you, Ms. G.? We can't *get* back to the gymnasium, and even if we could, we couldn't get from there to the plant room, or the walk-in fridge, or the ballroom, or any of it—the rooms *aren't in the same places*! How hard is that to figure out?"

"Calm down, Brianna! There's no need to get hysterical—I know you've had a traumatic day, and this is a very confusing house, but we need to keep our heads."

"*I am keeping my head!*" Brianna all but screamed. "You're the one who's gone completely mental! 'The ballroom is connected to the walk-in fridge on the other side of the gymnasium'—what sense does that even make? Did this place *look* like a convention centre when we came in? How could any of this stuff be up here? Think about it! This isn't a confusing house—it's *magic*! The doors move around and disappear as soon as you go through them—the view outside the windows doesn't make any sense—it was snowing outside the plant room, and now the sun is setting—look!" She flung an arm towards the dramatic clouds that showed through the dining-room windows, the pink light glinting on the silverware and wine glasses. "You're under a spell, Ms. G. Face it."

"All right, Brianna," said Ms. Gianelli, in a tone that said clearly, *I am humouring you.* "What do you suggest we do, mmm?"

Unfortunately, Brianna didn't have a good answer for this. Although it was plain to her what was going on, she had no idea why it was happening, still less what they could possibly do about it. Were they getting deeper into an enchantment with every door that they went through? Or were they *meant* to keep going through doors? If they stayed in one room, would something terrible happen? Would they disappear with the room, or suddenly find themselves in the building to which it actually belonged? Or was the whole thing quite random, and might they eventually pop out at the place where they had started if they just kept moving? On the whole, she preferred the idea of moving forward—but she thought they ought to be systematic about it, somehow.

"I think … " she said slowly, "I think we should look for clues. Look at these doors, for instance. None of them leads back to the place we just came from—well, none of them would. But is there something different about one of them?"

Ms. Gianelli frowned at her. "Different how, sweetie?"

"I don't know," Brianna said, deflated. "Just different." This was hopeless, she thought, looking at the doors. They were all the same.

But she hadn't realized how helpful Ms. Gianelli could be when she was trying to be patronizing. "That one has a glass doorknob," she said, pointing. "All the others are metal. Is that the kind of difference you mean, sweetie?"

"Yeah! Good one, Ms. G." Brianna brightened immediately. "Let's take that door."

The woman outside the door was not quite what Nick had been expecting. She looked about Rose's age, and was thin and freckled, with bright red hair pulled back into a severe pony tail. She looked businesslike.

"Morgan," she said, holding out a thin hand and giving

a firm handshake. "Ellen Morgan. I'm from Whitebeam. Is Rose around?"

"She's just gone upstairs—she should be back any minute. But I can show you … " He gestured towards Denise, as Ellen Morgan stepped inside the bakery.

"Ah, yes. Well, I'm glad you called me. I think I know this handiwork."

"It was a duel," Nick supplied, since Denise had fallen silent. "She killed her opponent. You know who he was?"

"No," said Ellen Morgan. "I know the smith who created the sword. I must speak to him about vetting his customers more carefully. He shouldn't be selling to Folk who make a habit of attacking humans. He knows that."

She approached Denise, but Denise, to Nick's surprise, rose stiffly from her chair and backed away.

"You're another of them," she said. "Aren't you?"

Ellen Morgan's pale eyebrows went up. "What makes you think that?"

"You look like them."

Morgan smiled. She did look like them, Nick saw. Her ears, visible because of her tightly pulled-back hair, were distinctly pointed. Her eyes were glittering black without discernible pupils or irises. She had not looked that way when she walked through the door, but he wasn't particularly surprised. He had assumed she was something of the sort.

"It's very useful, being able to see through the glamour," said Morgan to Denise. "But you must trust me, all the same. It's because I'm another one like the fairy you fought that I can help. We are not all alike. We can choose to be hostile to humans or to be helpful. I have chosen to be helpful."

Denise sat back down. "You'll have to excuse me. I'm a little jumpy."

At first, Brianna's strategy of getting Ms. Gianelli to pick the doors seemed to be working. They weren't retracing their steps, but the rooms that they passed through started to become more and more normal. They passed through an office, and a sort of waiting room with fluorescent lights overhead, and beyond that there was a hallway that seemed like it might be part of a hotel, with ordinary hotel rooms on either side. Then they passed through a door at the far end that led to a concrete stairwell with red-painted railings, and Brianna got quite excited about the possibility that this was a way out. Here, however, Ms. Gianelli became convinced that they should go up the stairs instead of down.

"Ms. G., we want to get out," said Brianna. "And out has to mean down."

"We're looking for the bathroom, sweetie—remember? And look!" She pointed to a sign on the concrete wall bearing male and female figures and an arrow pointing straight up.

"I don't need the bathroom any more, Ms. G. Let's just go back down to the bakery."

"Don't be silly. We came up here to get you cleaned up, didn't we? And we've found the bathroom we were looking for."

"No, we haven't—we've found a sign about bathrooms. Or something. Who knows what that even means in a place like this? And we'd have to go through another door to get to these 'bathrooms,' and then we might end up anywhere."

"You mustn't worry so much about these things, Brianna. I'm sure that if the bathrooms aren't at the top of the stairs, there will be another sign to point us the way."

And Ms. Gianelli set off resolutely up the concrete steps.

Brianna stood on the landing, feeling ready to cry with frustration. She was so sure that if they only went down, they would end up back where they started. There hadn't been another staircase anywhere else. But she couldn't just abandon Ms. Gianelli to wander around here forever. Reluctantly she started up the stairs after her.

As she was halfway up the first flight and had reached the landing where the stairs turned, she heard a noise below, like a rattling of beads. She leaned over the red railing to look down at the concrete stairs spiralling away below. Someone was coming out onto a landing several flights down; Brianna could just see the top of a head, and thought she recognized the baker, Rose.

She opened her mouth to call down to the woman, and then the whole staircase seemed to turn inside out. The red railings unhooked themselves from the walls and twisted upwards; the concrete steps rose and flattened out like an escalator. The person below Brianna disappeared, and the bang of a door from above told her that Ms. Gianelli was gone too. Brianna was alone in a low-ceilinged, concrete-floored room full of metal pipes covered in flaking red paint. It looked like a hasty, unconvincing sketch of a furnace room or the inside of a submarine.

Brianna stamped her feet and let out a miserable wail.

"Why is this happening? Why is this *all* happening to *me*?" Her voice echoed metallically among the pipes.

She felt a little better for her outburst, and pulled herself together enough to look around for a door. There was one, down at the end of the room, painted red like the pipes. She hauled it open and stepped through.

Ellen Morgan's cure for Denise was elegant in its simplic-
ity. She brought out of her bag something that looked like
a wooden crochet hook. (Nick wouldn't have known that
was what it looked like, but Denise made the comment, and
Morgan merely smiled.) She poked Denise gently with this
instrument a couple of times, and eventually hooked up a
pale green, sticky-looking filament, which she pulled out
delicately until it was arm's length, then began winding into
a ball, exactly as if it were yarn. She had a hefty, fist-sized
ball by the time the other end of the green filament came
out, with a slight, sticky pop. She coiled it neatly onto the
outside of the ball and held the whole thing up critically.

"Fine work," she remarked, "although put to a reprehen-
sible use." She popped the green ball into her bag along with
the crochet hook. "I didn't discuss payment with Rose," she
said, turning to Nick. "But I have to be on my way now. I'll
take a pie for the time being. Whatever you have on hand."

"She's done some pecan pies this morning. I'll go put one
in a box for you." He was trying not to look at Denise. She
was still half tree, and he wondered whether she was just
going to have to stay that way.

"Don't worry," said Morgan, glancing between the two
of them. "It will wear off—it may take a week, so you might
want to stay out of public places until then."

"You can totally stay here," said Nick, relieved.

"Thank you," said Denise.

Nick had thought of something else. "Do you have a
card?" he asked Morgan. "It's just that I have a f– an ac-
quaintance who might want to talk to you."

Morgan smiled her enigmatic smile, and dug in her bag
for her card. She had resumed her human appearance—

when, Nick hadn't noticed. "Is your friend in some difficulty?"

"She's … uh … wondering about her heritage, and what to do about it. I was just thinking that you might be able to give her some advice."

"I'd certainly try." She handed him the card.

"Cool." He stuffed it in his pocket. "I'll get you the pie. Then I'll go upstairs and see what's happened to Rose."

Brianna stood in the middle of a deserted shopping mall, planning her strategy. The rooms had been getting steadily bigger now. Before this there had been an empty cafeteria, and before that a movie theatre, with no one in the seats and a slapstick comedy with Chinese subtitles playing on the screen. The darkened mall was the most frightening so far, but she could imagine worse possibilities. A subway tunnel? The tiger enclosure at the zoo? She now had the distinct impression that someone was trying to scare her—or worse. But she had a plan.

The stores in the mall were not shuttered—that was partly what made it so creepy—so she went into a clothing store and made for the mirrored door of the fitting rooms. She turned the handle and pulled it casually open, grabbing the inner doorknob as she did so. Beyond was musty dimness; she felt stones underfoot. It might have been the basement of a castle or something. For a moment she felt a slight tug of curiosity. But now was not the time.

She still had her hand on the knob of the fitting room door as it swung closed behind her. She was careful not to look at it as she heard it click softly into place. Then she turned swiftly, twisting the knob and pushing with all her might.

The door was fading into the stone wall even as she turned toward it, but she had caught it in time. There was a strange ripping sound, and for a moment the lines of the door bulged and jiggled like a cartoon. Then it gave way, and the door swung limply inwards. Brianna stumbled through into a sunlit bedroom.

Compared to the places she had just been, it was a comfortingly ordinary room. Appealing, even. There were anime posters on the walls—mostly giant robots and historical samurai things, but there was one from *InuYasha*— and shelves of manga in Japanese. But the most reassuring thing about the room was that it was not empty. There was someone sleeping on the futon in the middle of the floor, mostly an indistinct shape curled up under the comforter, but with a head turned away from her on the pillow amid a swirl of black hair, and a light-brown foot poking out at the bottom.

Brianna stood holding the door, which felt loose and rubbery in her hand, unsure what would be the politest thing to do. Before she had a chance to decide, the person under the covers uncurled, snakelike, and sat up to stare at her.

He was a boy, which fit with the anime posters, although he was older than she would have expected, maybe almost twenty. He could actually have been Japanese, and even with his eyes barely open and his hair mussed up from sleeping on it, he was gorgeous. He could have played Yoshimori in a live-action version of *Different Hearts*, Brianna thought. Or Kenji from *Blood Red*, if he cut his hair—but he really shouldn't cut his hair. He was glaring at her.

"Who are you?" he demanded. "What are you doing

here?" The perfect voice for Kenji, too—a bit too deep for Yoshimori.

It occurred to her suddenly that it was not at all clear that she was still, in any meaningful way, in Toronto at all, and that she should be relieved to hear Kenji speaking English. She became businesslike.

"I'm Brianna Baker. Nick from the bakery downstairs told me to come up here to look for the washroom, but I'm lost. The rooms keep moving around."

To her unspeakable relief, he nodded as if this made perfect sense. "They do that," he said.

He kicked free of the comforter and got to his feet. He was quite tall. He was wearing shorts and a tank top that showed off the compact muscles of his shoulders—he would definitely be good in all the scenes where Yoshimori ended up with his shirt off. And, to Brianna's complete delight, he took down a blue-and-white yukata from a hook on the closet door and threw it on.

"Why did that fool tell you to come up here?" he wondered aloud. "There is a bathroom downstairs. He should have known you would get lost up here. He is such a fool."

She didn't think Nick was a fool, but she wasn't going to argue.

"Do you live here?" she asked.

"Mm." He turned the handle of the door, which Brianna had let fall closed behind her. "I am—" He stopped.

He had opened the door and seen what was on the other side. He stared for a moment.

"What?" He sounded perplexed. He leaned through the door and looked up and down the long, white marble room full of pillars outside. "*What?*" he repeated. This time it sounded as if he were actually addressing someone or something outside the door. He got no answer, though, and he turned back to glare at Brianna.

"How long is it like this?" he demanded.

"Like that? It wasn't like that just now." Her heart sank slightly. Maybe he didn't know what was going on after all. But he had seemed to know Nick, and the bakery; that had to be a good sign. "It was a mall when I came through just now."

His eyebrows went up. "A mall? And how did you get *there*?"

Her heart sank further. "Um ... I just came through a door. From a cafeteria. Not a cafeteria that was part of the mall—like a school cafeteria."

To her surprise, he nodded again as though this was making sense. "And before that it was something else and something else? What was it to begin with? When you first came up the stairs, through the door ... no, the curtain— the door got destroyed. What was it after that?"

"Uh, just a hallway. Like ... like an apartment building, with carpet on the floor, and metal doors. You know."

"No ... that's not really part of it, either. There is a hall-way, but it is not like that. That's very strange."

"You're telling me!"

"You came up here by yourself? That stupid Nick sent you up here by yourself?"

"No, no—Nick didn't send me up by myself at all. He said ... he was going to come up to show me where the bathroom was, but then he thought it would be better for Cristina to show me—you know, the, uh, vampire. She came upstairs with me, and Ms. Gianelli too. She's the vice principal at my mother's school. You wouldn't know her. But they both got lost. Cristina just went through a door ahead of us and never came out, but Ms. Gianelli and I wandered around for a long time, through all these different rooms, and then finally we came to these stairs—not the stairs that we came up the first time, but different stairs— and I thought we should go down, but Ms. G. wanted to go up, and then … we got separated. I don't know what's happened to her. You don't think … she couldn't be lost *forever*, could she? Could *we*?"

"No … " He looked thoughtful. "No, we are still in 7C, of course. She would be too, and Cristina. And … Rose, I think. I can't tell … I don't know how we would get to them. Something has gone very wrong. I think I know why, though."

He let the door swing shut on the marble pillars, and went over to the computer on his desk and tapped its keyboard to wake it up. After a moment, he nodded.

"I think," he said reluctantly, "this is a little bit my fault."

He rubbed his hands over his face and pushed his hair back behind his ears. Brianna felt her heart turning to ice inside her.

Nick stared down the length of what he could only assume was a hall in some kind of Japanese palace. The walls were made of gilded and painted panels between beams of glowing dark wood, the floor covered in tatami mats, the ceiling divided into squares and gilded to within an inch of its life. There were no windows that he could see; all the light was coming from behind him. He turned around. There was a wall of sliding rice-paper screens, with no sign of the doorway he had come in by.

"What the actual fuck?" he said aloud. Then, after thinking about it for a moment, turning back toward the gilded hall, "Tac-*ky*!"

A door at the far end of the hall slid open almost immediately, but the person who entered was not Tacky, though she looked a bit like him. She also looked like she belonged in the Japanese palace; she wore layers of elaborate kimonos, and had bizarre painted-on eyebrows, and came through the door sideways on her knees, the way that he had seen people do in Japanese period films. Nick froze, waiting for her to notice him and scream, then wasn't sure whether he should be relieved or dismayed when she looked straight through him.

"Okay ... so I'm not really here, or *she's* not really here, or this whole thing isn't real, or ... huh."

He turned back to the rice-paper screens, and slid one open. He found himself looking out on the children's section of the Sanderson Public Library. That was odd, certainly, but it seemed preferable, just on a practical level, to medieval Japan, or whatever this place was. He stepped through.

There were people in the library, but as the door Nick had come through looked, on this side, like the door to the men's washroom, none of them took much notice of him. He looked out through the windows onto the corner of Dundas and Bathurst. It was pouring rain. That was weird too, because it hadn't been raining when he came in—hadn't even looked like rain.

He was standing there considering this when a toddler clutching a picture book ran up to him. She stopped and craned her neck to stare at him, and he looked down at her. She was a pretty girl, with a pale, pink-cheeked face, black hair in pigtails, and dark, not-quite-Asian eyes. She held her book up to Nick, serenely expectant. It had a wolf on the cover.

"Jasmine!" came a woman's voice. Nick looked up, startled. It was Rose's voice.

And there was Rose, getting up from a chair by a table in the kids' section, laughing, coming over to scoop up the little girl, who went on looking at Nick over Rose's shoulder. But Rose herself hadn't seen Nick at all.

He made for the front doors, dodging his way around library patrons, not wanting to find out what it would feel like for one of them to walk through him. And then the door wouldn't open to let him out.

"Oh, for the love of—"

He dashed back to the men's washroom, less careful now that he was panicking, and a librarian did walk right through him, and it felt just as stomach-churningly awful as he had imagined it might.

The door to the men's washroom opened onto a marble museum atrium full of men with shaggy hair and brown suits and women in loud polyester dresses. Nick shrank out of their way against a column, with a moan of desperation.

He found himself looking up at a huge poster advertising one of the museum's current exhibits, *The Art of the Momoyama Period*. Reproduced on the poster was an ink-painting of an androgynous, beautiful figure, turning away from the viewer in a swirl of draperies, looking back over one shoulder, long hair drawn forward over the other shoulder to show off the white snake that writhed between stylized clouds over the back of his red kimono. It was unmistakably Takehiko. He held a sheathed sword in one hand, and the other hand was poised as if about to draw it, his long fingers rendered in delicate brush-strokes. The expression on his face was distinctly unfriendly.

Staring up at the poster of Tacky, Nick forced himself to think about what he had just seen in the library. Rose's daughter. Rose's clearly half-Asian daughter. Rose's daughter who had been able to see Nick when no one else in the library had, not even the other children: Rose's daughter who was, it would seem, not entirely human. Much as he would have liked to, he couldn't pretend he didn't see what all that added up to.

He was accustomed to thinking of Rose as older than Tacky, but of course she wasn't really. All the same, imagining the two of them together ... he couldn't do it, didn't *want* to do it.

Had they been a couple? They didn't act as though they had been a couple. What had it been, then? A one-night stand? "Friends with benefits"? Surely not. He didn't want to think about it, so he was going to stop.

Rose had an ex-husband, he knew that much. Was that why her marriage had broken up? Had she cheated on her husband with Takehiko? Of course it was easy to see why Rose would have fallen for him ... (Wait, what? Where had *that* thought come from?)

He looked down finally from the poster, and realized that the real Takehiko was standing in the nearby entrance to the museum gift-shop, looking at him quizzically. He was wearing his blue yukata over his pyjamas, and he was barefoot. The tourists were paying no more attention to him than to Nick—in fact, as Nick looked, a pair of women in bellbottoms walked straight through Tacky, and he didn't so much as flinch. By coincidence, his hair was pulled forward over his shoulder in the same way as in the picture. Nick looked up at it one last time. Sure enough, you could see the outline of one ear, and it was just slightly pointed at the top.

Nick made his way from the safety of his column to the

doorway where Tacky was standing. "What the fuck is going on?"

"The network is down."

"The *who*?"

"The *net-work*," Tacky repeated, unimpressed. "On the computer."

"Yeah, I know what a network is. What does it have to do with any of this time-travel bullshit?"

"Time travel?" Now it was Tacky who looked puzzled.

"Look around you—we're in the '70s! We're in … " He paused for a moment, listening to the people around him. "We're in the UK, I think." Then he spotted the logo on a sign behind Takehiko. "Oh. The British Museum. But I guess you know that. You're in an exhibit, apparently."

Tacky looked up at another instance of the poster, hanging between the columns behind Nick, and his eyes widened for an instant as if in pain. What was that? Nick wondered. PTSD or something? Maybe he should have been more sensitive.

"Come," said Tacky, quickly recovering his composure. He stepped back through the gift-shop doorway, gesturing.

Nick followed him, and like flicking a switch, the British Museum gift-shop from forty years ago blinked out and was replaced by Takehiko's bedroom in 7C.

Tacky shook himself slightly and shut the door behind them. "You were the easiest to find," he said. "Cristina I could find too, but it is harder to get to her. Rose is somewhere inside, but I can't tell where. Rose is confusing these days."

You're telling me, Nick thought. Wait—had that sounded like an ex-boyfriend kind of thing to say? But no. He wasn't going to think about it.

"Okay, so here's what happened from my point of view,"

said Nick. "I came through the door at the top of the stairs, and I was in … I don't know, Japan, I guess, in the Middle Ages, or—well, probably the seventeenth century, where you're from. In some kind of palace. Were you ever in a palace? I'm guessing I was plugged into your timeline somehow."

"Go on," said Tacky unhelpfully.

"Well, then I opened the door from there and came out in Toronto, but a couple of years into the future. And nobody could see me, and they walked through me and stuff. And when I tried to go out the door, like outside, it wouldn't open."

"No, it wouldn't."

"So I went back out the door I came in by, and ended up where you found me. So what's going on?"

"I said. The network is down. It's … security. It protects the house. And when the house is not protected, the apartment gets … thinks everyone is an intruder. So it is making up new rooms to confuse them."

"Okay, that makes sense, I guess. But why the time travelling?"

"I don't know," Tacky admitted. "I don't think it was doing that at first, and I don't know why it started."

"So why is the network down? Do you know?"

Tacky nodded. "The power is out."

"Still? It's still out? You didn't fix the damn fuse."

"No."

It was not as satisfying as he had expected it to be, discovering that Takehiko had done something wrong.

"I was going to," Tacky said, "but when I went down to the basement, there wasn't a new one. I asked Cristina where do you get a fuse, and she said a hardware store. She told me where there is one."

"She … told you where … "

"It was sunny. She couldn't go."

"So you were gonna go by yourself?"

Tacky had stuck his hands into the sleeves of his yukata and looked unhappy. "I thought maybe."

"But you didn't."

"No."

"Well, that's okay. Next time, just tell me, though. Like, I mean, there's no reason not to tell me."

Takehiko nodded. "I am very sorry."

"It's okay, man. Whatever. You didn't know it was going to do this."

"No."

"So we have to somehow get out of the house, while it's all crazy like this, and get to the hardware store for a fuse?"

Tacky shook his head. "Not all the power is gone, right?"

"Right. Just that one circuit in the kitchen. So if we plugged the modem into a different outlet … What about the other people, though—Brianna, and that idiotic woman? You don't know where they are?"

"No," Tacky admitted. "Brianna, she came in here, but something scared her—I don't know what, something about me—and she ran out again. The other woman, I don't know who you mean."

"Ms. Gianelli. I'll bet she's the real problem, actually. She was *way* in denial about everything—I think the Folk may have put a hex on her. I could see where that kind of thing might make the apartment freak out. But is it safe to bring the network back online with them out there? I mean, could they get trapped?"

Tacky frowned. "Nothing like this has happened before. I don't know."

"So we should probably find them first."

"Yes."

"And how *in the fuck* do we do that?"

Tacky looked thoughtfully up at the ceiling. "The attic," he said after a moment, with a decided nod.

"The what? There's no attic. Is there?"

"Not really." He went over to his closet, shrugging off the yukata. Nick looked away. When he looked back, Tacky was zipping up his jeans. He said, "There is a space between the ceiling and the roof, and if we can get into it, we are not exactly in the apartment, but we should be able to see down into its magic. Come. It is easier just to see if it works."

He sprang up onto his desk, and from there to the top of one of his bookshelves, and casually punched a hole in the ceiling as if it were made of paper. He tore the edge of the hole to make it bigger, folding it up inside itself, while Nick watched in fascination. Then he pulled himself up through the hole and looked back down at Nick, long hair dangling.

"Well, come on!"

"Um, okay." Nick scrambled awkwardly onto the book-shelf, afraid he was going to knock it over. He grabbed Tacky's hands and was hauled easily up into the space above the ceiling.

It was dim, and hot like an attic, and you could sense the roof above you, but the space seemed to have no limits; it stretched off into the darkness in all directions, impossibly huge, a network of rooms with no ceilings. You could, as Tacky had surmised, see down into them. And up here there were only the tops of the walls, and rickety things like lad-ders of bamboo stretching across them, and sinister black fissures between chains of rooms that snaked off into the dark distance. Nick and Tacky were perched on the top of the wall between Tacky's bedroom and the British Museum.

"Holy cow," said Nick, looking around. "This hasn't been up here all the time, has it?"

"No," said Tacky witheringly, "of course not. It's not real. It's only … to make you see it."

"Like a projection?" He looked at the bamboo ladders; they had an ancient-Japan look to them that didn't really belong to 7C. "Never mind. It's probably better if you don't explain it—I might not be able to see it any more, or something, if I know how it works."

Takehiko gave him a disgusted look but didn't say he thought otherwise. He unfolded himself from where he was crouched on the wall, and began to walk along it, toward another room that branched off at a weird angle from the British Museum lobby.

"Mm. It is what I thought."

"What is what you thought?"

"The old rooms are all here, still connected. You can see where they have gone."

"Uh … right." Nick tried to sound as if he understood that.

He followed Tacky along the top of the wall above the British Museum, trying to ignore the dark chasm that plunged away on the opposite side.

"So the computer network—who set it up, anyway? Rose?"

Tacky shook his head. "A guy."

"A guy?"

"Yes. A guy. I can't talk about him."

"Why not?"

"I can't talk about that. I can't talk about why I can't talk about him—that would be the same as talking about him."

"That doesn't make *any* sense."

Nick had reached the corner of the British Museum wall,

and Tacky had set out across one of the bamboo ladders over the top of the Sanderson library. "It is not suppose to make sense," he said without looking back. "It is a curse."

"Oh," said Nick. Why, he wondered irritably, did he so often feel like he understood his own life about as well as the average guy on the street who thought there was no such thing as werewolves? It didn't seem fair.

He followed Tacky across the bamboo ladder, treading much more gingerly and dropping to hands and knees in the middle, so that by the time he got to the opposite wall, Tacky was already two rooms away. As Nick got to his feet above the Japanese palace room, he saw Tacky leap lightly from the top of a wall across one of the black fissures onto another wall.

"I think I can see the kitchen," Tacky called.

"Great!" Nick tried to sound enthusiastic. He wished he couldn't picture himself falling away into one of the chasms, arms and legs flailing hopelessly, while the words GAME OVER scrolled across the scene. Then he had an idea.

Takehiko turned in surprise to find the wolf loping easily along the wall behind him.

"*Okami-kun*!" He laughed.

The wolf thought, *I have seen him laugh more often than that boy Nick. I think he likes me better.* He wasn't entirely sure why he didn't find this thought more satisfying.

"Why do you have Nick's boot?" Takehiko asked, tipping his head to one side curiously.

The wolf unclamped his jaws from the boot and snuffled at it.

"Ah, for the scent," said Takehiko, nodding. "So that you can change back?"

He was smart, that one.

"The kitchen is over there." Takehiko pointed across a wide black gap of nothingness to a lit box beyond.

The wolf picked up the boot again. He hunkered down, bunching his shoulders and his hindquarters, and jumped. He heard a startled cry from the boy who wasn't human, and the next moment he realized he hadn't cleared the black nothing, and he was falling into it.

A hand closed on the scruff of his neck, an arm scooped around his ribcage, and Takehiko twisted impossibly in mid-air to push off the outside of the kitchen-box. The wolf could feel him straining every muscle to flip them up onto the top of the wall. Takehiko dropped the wolf and sank down into a crouch. Only then did the wolf notice that he had let go of the boot.

He flattened his ears back and folded his tail abjectly between his legs. Takehiko waved a dismissive hand.

You don't think you are still Nick, he said, *but you are.* "That was a completely Nick thing to do."

The wolf was mystified by this.

Here is what we need to do, said Takehiko after a moment. *I must stay up here, for now, to sustain this construction—if I were to go back down into 7C, it might all change, and if I leave this spot, we might not find our way back to the kitchen. You go along the top of the walls and look for the others. When you find them, drop down into the room, and take them out a door—it will lead back here. Do you understand?*

The wolf growled in what he meant to signify assent, then remembered that he could talk to Takehiko.

Yes, sir.

The boy's eyebrows went up. *Good.* "Don't try to fly again, okay?"

No, sir. I'm very sorry, sir.

The wolf set off along the tops of the walls and across

the bamboo ladders, above strings of strange human hab-
itations, looking for the tops of familiar heads. There were
people in a few of the rooms he passed over, but not the
people he sought, and most were empty altogether.

Takehiko's words bothered him. Still Nick? But that was
impossible. Nick was an adolescent, stupid and unformed,
whereas the wolf was four years old, fully grown and ma-
ture. If he'd had a mate, he could have fathered litters by
now, and if he were human, he'd have been a big man, with
a beard and everything, not a weedy teenager. Takehiko
was smart, certainly, but here he didn't know what he was
talking about, and that was that.

The wolf almost missed the first of the people he was
supposed to be looking for, because the room she was in
was pitch dark and filled with wooden boxes. Coffins, in
fact—that's what they were, human coffins, and down in a
corner of the room, sitting with her knees drawn up and
her arms wrapped around them, was a human. Or, well,
Cristina. She was more or less human, as far as the wolf
was concerned. She walked and talked like a human, and
smelled human, just sort of stale.

He gave a low whine to get her attention. He could
bark like a dog, but he considered it beneath him. Cristina
looked up, confused and suspicious. The wolf pawed at the
top of the wall and wagged his tail, but her eyes slid right
past him as if she couldn't see him at all. Finally he realized
that she couldn't, because from her perspective, the ceiling
was in the way. He bounded down into the room, landing
on the floor between the stacks of coffins. Cristina shrieked
and jumped up.

"Nick? *Futu-ți Paștele mă-tii*! You scared me!"

The wolf growled and shook himself irritably. He wished
Nick would explain things to these people.

"What are you doing here, jumping out of the ceiling? Ugh! Why am I asking questions to a wolf?"

Go out the door, Takehiko had said. The wolf prowled around the piles of coffins, looking for a door.

Cristina followed him, still talking. "I don't know what happened—do you? When we came upstairs, there was a hallway I'd never seen before, and one door led to a disco, but it was empty. So I look for the rest of the apartment, and instead I get myself trapped in this awful room of windows, and it was sunny, the door disappeared, and I had to crawl around the edge where there was shadow, and when I got in here, I said I am not moving until somebody comes to find me. I didn't think it would be you," she added.

The wolf had found the door, and took a swipe at the handle with his front paws. It was a slippery glass knob, and he couldn't twist it to pop the catch. He dropped back to the floor.

"You should not do that," said Cristina before he could try again. "You don't know where it might lead."

The wolf looked up at her, teeth bared. He realized this part would have been easier for Nick, and the thought annoyed him. He should have picked up something else in the kitchen that held the boy's scent, so that he could have found him, allowed him to take over.

"Look," Cristina said, reaching for the doorknob. "I will show you."

She pulled the door open, and the wolf skipped confidently through. Takehiko had told him it would take him to the kitchen, and he trusted Takehiko.

Beyond the door was not the kitchen but a weird, twilit hallway, lined with dense green stalks and rustling leaves: a passage made of living bamboo. The wolf was not disconcerted by this, because the whole thing carried Takehiko's unmistakeable scent. It would lead to the kitchen, he felt sure. But Cristina required some convincing. He tried wagging his tail and perking up his ears. He tried bounding away down the passage and then bounding back and looking at her expectantly. He tried barking like a dog. He tried growling. He knew she could tell what he was getting at. She said, "I'm not going in there. You're crazy!" She said, "Come out of there, Nick! You don't know where it goes." He wanted to bite her.

He thought about running down to the other end, to the kitchen, to turn into Nick and come back to reason with her, but he was afraid if he left, she would give up on him and shut the door, and then he wouldn't be able to get back. Finally, when he had just about decided to give up on her and leave her in her dark room full of coffins, she decided to dive into the hallway to try to grab him and haul him back, and, as he had fully expected, the door swung shut behind her and disappeared.

"Now look what you've done!" she wailed. "We'll be trapped in here until the sun comes up, and I will turn to dust! Dust!" She followed him down the bamboo passage, repeating variations on this theme, until they reached an archway that opened onto the 7C kitchen, and all she said was, "Huh."

The kitchen looked perfectly normal, except that the ceiling was gone. Instead you could look up into Takehiko's dark attic projection. And there was Takehiko himself, lounging elegantly on the top of the wall above the sink. The wolf whined happily and wagged his tail.

Well done, Okami-kun, said Takehiko.

It was difficult, the wolf admitted. *She didn't want to come.*

Now to find something that smelled of Nick. There was a

basket of laundry in the corner of the kitchen by the washing machine, but it was freshly washed, and when the wolf
sniffed it, all he could detect was a soapy, clean smell. He
headed for the pile of stuff by the entry, pulled out a bat-
tered and smelly sneaker, and loped back into the kitchen.
It occurred to him that Nick was going to be annoyed with
him for losing that boot; he recalled that the pair had been
Nick's favourite. Not that a wolf should have any understanding of that kind of thing. He brushed the thought away.

He bounded up onto the counter, and from there to the
top of the cupboards, and onto the wall beside Takehiko,
while Cristina began demanding an explanation of what
was going on. He loped along the top of the walls with the
sneaker dangling from his mouth, looking down into the
succession of strange rooms.

Ah, there she was: the girl, Brianna. The one who had
been inside the deer. She was slouched glumly on a pew
at the back of a small, white-painted church, conspicuous
by her T-shirt and jeans, which contrasted with the flowered hats and dresses worn by all the other women in the
pews. No one was paying attention to her, but that could
have been because they were too busy singing. The wolf,
who had no reason to understand music, being a wolf, felt
there was something familiar about the song. Back to business. Should he become Nick up here and then jump down
into the church? No, he decided; Nick would be useless
at getting down from the top of the wall, which was fairly
high. He prowled around for a suitable way down, and finally settled for jumping onto the top of the organ console.
The organist—another dark-skinned human in a flowered
hat—went right on playing, as the wolf had suspected she
would. He jumped from the organ to the floor, navigated

his way around the choir, and loped down the aisle toward Brianna's pew.

She had seen him, and got warily to her feet. He came level with her pew.

"Hi," she said. "They can't see you either, huh?"

He dropped the sneaker, which she eyed suspiciously. Maybe she thought he had eaten its owner. He realized she was being very brave, considering that the last time they met, she had been a deer, and he had sunk his teeth into her.

The scent of the sneaker was strong enough that the wolf didn't need to sniff at it to find the route back to Nick; the path was plain before him. But Nick, for the first time in his experience, was unwilling to come back. The wolf growled in perplexity. It was something to do with the place, he realized, something to do with …

He shook himself all over. He'd just had a wholly disquieting glimpse into Nick's thoughts: not a memory of things that Nick had previously thought, but a genuine insight into some convoluted human business that wolves definitely should not understand. It was of course wholly stupid, but worse than that, it was improper. He felt a strong desire to roll around in something to get the scent of it off him.

But there were more important things to worry about. Brianna was looking at him even more warily, obviously not being able to guess what he had been growling about, and not knowing whether she should think of him as friendly or not. The wolf did his best harmless-dog imitation (it might be demeaning, but it was undeniably useful) and lolloped away toward the big double doors at the back of the church. He left the useless smelly sneaker lying in the aisle.

After a moment, Brianna followed cautiously, and when the wolf wagged his tail and looked expectantly between her and the door handles, she hesitated only a moment before grasping one and hauling the door open. The wolf decided that he liked her.

Brianna followed the wolf at what she hoped was a safe distance—but who was she kidding? she'd seen him run—down the corridor of softly swaying bamboo stalks. It was so different from any of the other places she had found on the other side of the doors up here that she felt hopeful it was finally leading somewhere altogether new. More importantly, she trusted Nick.

She remembered seeing in a documentary on wolves how they rarely attacked people, in spite of the legends. Of course, considering that some of the legends—the ones about people who could turn into wolves—were obviously true, that wasn't as comforting as it might have been. But this wolf was Nick, and she trusted Nick.

The bamboo path ended, unexpectedly, in another room, this one a big, dimly lit kitchen. There was a perfectly normal fridge, a perfectly normal stove, and a perfectly normal table and chairs and cupboards. The blinds were all pulled down, and Cristina was sitting at the table, chin on her fist, doing a sudoku in the newspaper. There was something weird about the ceiling. Brianna looked up at it, and looked away again. It made her a bit dizzy.

The wolf had bounded past her across the kitchen to a little mudroom on the other side. She followed, afraid he was going to go through another door and disappear. She didn't want to be left alone with Cristina—not so much because she was a vampire as because she seemed useless.

But the wolf wasn't going through the door, and Brianna stopped short when she realized that he was gone, and Nick was kneeling amid the potted plants and umbrellas on the floor of the mudroom, totally naked.

She didn't really see much before she looked away, just enough to carry away the impression that his skin was very white, and he was bony thin, the way all the guy characters were drawn in *Mercury Kiss*. She had an ongoing debate with her friend Tina about it, but she'd always kind of liked the way the guys were drawn in *Mercury Kiss*.

"Sorry, sorry!" Brianna and Nick chorussed, and Cristina laughed.

"Can I get you some clothes?" Brianna suggested, spotting a washer and dryer and laundry basket across the kitchen.

"Uh, thanks—I'm good."

She looked back at him. He had wrapped himself in a big green army coat that he had got out of the closet. His hair was sticking up wildly, and he was blushing, and he looked—well, he looked adorable.

She sensed movement, or a shadow or something, and looked up, and choked back a scream. Perched on top of the wall, in the dim, weird space above where the ceiling should have been, was the Japanese boy. He was dressed in ordinary clothes now, jeans and a black T-shirt, and his hair had fallen forward to hide his pointed ears.

She grabbed Nick's sleeve. "What's he doing here?" she asked, jabbing a finger.

"Huh? Oh, that's Takehiko. The fuck you doing, man, appearing out of nowhere and scaring people?"

The Japanese boy raised his eyebrows. "At least I have clothes on."

Brianna edged away into the kitchen, still keeping a hold on Nick's sleeve. He gave her a puzzled look.

"He's one of *them*," she explained.

"Uh … "

"I saw his ears. He's a fay."

"Kind of, but he's cool, though. He's a yokai, actually. That's—"

"I know what that is. I read tons of manga. And that's *not* comforting. Some of them are totally evil. Plus … how do I know he's not using glamour on me like Cian? He's got pointed ears, and he's way too pretty. I mean, he looks pretty to *me*—how do I know what he looks like to anybody else?"

"Oh, no, he totally does look like that. I mean, he's very … he's, uh … " His voice trailed off, and his face began to get red again. Just as Brianna was deciding that he was so embarrassed that she couldn't help believing him, he added: "I wouldn't worry about it. He wouldn't try to glamour *you*—he's gay."

"Ohhhh," said Brianna. She looked up at Takehiko with a renewed interest. His face was stony, but she thought his eyebrows had gone up a fraction. "I'm sorry I ran away," she said. "One of the fay tried to kill my mom, and so … "

"It's all good," said Nick. "Right, Tacky?"

"Mm." Takehiko nodded. "I am sorry to scare you."

"Tacky lives in 7C too—that's where we are, the apartment above the bakery," Nick explained. "This is really our kitchen, but the rest of the apartment has gone haywire—we think it's because we blew a fuse, and our security network went down." He went to the counter and pulled the plug on an ordinary-looking high-speed modem. "So all the rooms are switching up randomly as, like, a backup security measure. I'm gathering up everybody and bringing them back to the kitchen before we restart the network and the rooms go back to normal. If you, uh, follow that."

"I guess so. You guys live together?" said Brianna, looking between Nick and Takehiko.

Cristina snorted.

"Ye-es," said Nick. "Like roommates."

"Oh." Brianna tried not to sound disappointed. That would have been too cool. They were both so cute. "And … why is your apartment like this?"

Nick looked surprised. "Actually, I have no idea." He looked at Cristina. "Do you know?"

"No."

"Tacky?"

Takehiko shrugged. "Not really."

There was a pause.

"Aren't you *curious*?" Brianna finally burst out.

They looked at one another.

"I don't know," Nick said. "After a while, you kind of get used to things."

The others nodded in agreement.

"So … what do we do now?" Brianna asked. "And can I help?"

"I've got to go back up and look for the others," said Nick. "I think I might just do it as me. The wolf is really getting to be a pain. He's leaving my shoes all over the place, and he had some kind of existential crisis when I didn't want to change back in that church. I know nobody could see me, but fuck, it's still a church—I'm not gonna pop up naked in the aisle in the middle of a congregation singing 'Were you there when they crucified my Lord.' But wolf-me is all like, religion is the opiate of the masses or some shit."

Cristina glanced up from her sudoku to give him a look of almost respectful awe. "How sad is that? Your multi-personality is more rationalist than you are."

Nick rolled his eyes. "What-the-fuck-ever."

"What was the church?" Takehiko asked from his perch on top of the wall.

"I don't know, Baptist or something? You going to come down from there, or do you enjoy hovering over us like a gargoyle?"

"I told you, Stupid, I have to stay up here to keep it all working."

"It was my grandmother's church," Brianna said, to get the conversation back on track. "I think it was in the past, when my mom was a little girl. I probably could have seen her and my uncle, and my grandparents, if I'd gone up to the front, where they always sat—but somebody walked through me when they were taking up the collection, and it was so gross I sat down at the back and tried not to get near people."

Nick looked up at Takehiko. "If that was Brianna's mom's timeline, do you think that means she's in the apartment?"

Takehiko nodded.

"She probably came upstairs looking for me," said Brianna guiltily. "I've been gone a long time."

"I shouldn't have left her alone downstairs," said Nick.

"It's not your fault, you've been awesome. Can I come help you look for her? Please? I'd be useful—I'd probably recognize places from her past and stuff, which might help."

"Yeah, except that the places and people don't seem to match up. How do you feel about heights?"

"Heights? Like, up above the ceiling? That's nothing!"

"Yeah, but there's like these bottomless pits too, though."

"I know what," she said. "How about you change into the wolf, and I can come with you and do the talking. And I can bring some clothes, so if you need to change back, you'll have something to wear."

Nick looked impressed. "That's actually a really good idea."

He went over to the laundry basket, holding the front of

his coat closed, and pulled out a pair of pants and a T-shirt at random.

"I think those are pyjamas," Takehiko remarked. He had strolled over from the other side of the room and was lying along the top of the wall above the washer and dryer now, propped on one elbow.

"Shut up," said Nick, handing the clothes to Brianna. "You can put them in my bag—here." He grabbed a beat-up messenger bag and dumped stuff out of it. A textbook and binder flopped on the floor, and a couple of chewed pens bounced and rolled. He held the bag out by its strap, the other hand still holding the front of his coat.

"Great," she said, stuffing the clothes inside and wondering whether to point out that he hadn't included any underwear. She decided she didn't have any particular need to go around carrying his underwear, so she wouldn't mention it.

And then he changed form. One moment he was just Nick, cute in a pitiful kind of way in his oversized coat and bare feet, then he was two things at once, or nothing at all—a snarl, a flash of green eyes, dissolving into a wisp of magic—and then the coat plopped heavily onto the floor, and the wolf skipped sideways out from under it.

"Wow!" said Brianna. "That's amazing. I didn't realize you could just *do* that."

The wolf looked up at her and swished his tail modestly.

He could get easily up onto the top of the wall, but she had to clamber onto the counter and be hauled up by Takehiko. Then she saw what Nick had meant about bottomless pits. They were a bit frightening, but by this time she couldn't back out without looking like a coward, and she was determined to help.

"Creepy," she remarked aloud.

"I think Rose is that way," said Takehiko, pointing along one crazy, narrow path of wall-tops.

"You can sense her?" Brianna asked.

He nodded curtly, but he was frowning. "There is something … I can tell that she is there, but … "

"Do you think she might be in the past, like my mom?"

He gave her a look of surprised respect. "It might be that," he admitted.

"Well, we'll go see," she said, because the wolf had already started to prowl along the walls in that direction. She hurried carefully after him.

They passed above an office full of empty grey cubicles, something that looked like a school auditorium—it was dark, and hard to tell—and finally arrived above a gym full of mats and balance beams and little girls in leotards practicing gymnastic routines. There were a few adults near the door, and Brianna thought one of them looked like the woman from the bakery. She looked down at the wolf. To her surprise, his ears were laid back, and he was growling at something in the gym.

Brianna looked down again and saw that one of the little girls had stopped in the middle of her balance beam and stood with her hands on her hips, looking straight up at them. She had to be a few years younger than Brianna, but she was tall for her age, with shiny black hair in two long braids, and very white skin.

"No," she said firmly, glaring up at them. "I'm having fun."

"Sorry?" said Brianna, taking in the fact that nobody else in the gym seemed to have noticed the girl talking to the ceiling.

"I'm not going back," the girl said, crossing her arms and

tossing her head so that her braids swung behind her. "You can't make me."

Brianna glanced down at the wolf—Nick—but if he knew what was going on, he had no way of communicating it to her.

"Are you Rose?" Brianna suggested. It was the only thing she could think of. Maybe they were in the past, and the woman by the door was actually Rose's mother.

"Are you an idiot?" the girl asked humorously.

Out of the corner of her eye, Brianna saw one of the women by the door doing something with a smartphone—okay, so not the past.

"Whatever," she said. "We're not here for you. We're only interested in Rose." Who wasn't looking in their direction or behaving like she knew anything odd was going on. In fact, she was talking with one of the other women. And hadn't she been …

"You can't have her," the girl said smugly.

Pregnant. Rose had been pregnant. The woman by the door wasn't. Brianna began to get an idea of what was going on. She looked down at Nick again.

"Do you think you should change back so you can talk to her?" she suggested in a whisper.

He dipped his head in a wolf-style nod.

"I won't let you near her!" the girl sang out from below. "I'm having fun. I don't want to go back to being a baby—a boring, not-even-born-yet baby. I *prefer* being grown up."

"It's okay, though," said Brianna, casually slinging the bag off her shoulder and lowering it to the top of the wall beside Nick. "You can stay here, being grown up. It's just your mom who needs to come with us."

"I'm *inside* my mom, you incredible thicko! And I'm not going *anywhere* with you."

She stuck her arms out in front of her, as if grasping an invisible steering-wheel, and gave it a violent jerk to the right. The whole gym shuddered and began to move, swinging away to the right, and the wall where Brianna and the wolf were standing began to peel apart down the middle, a black fissure crackling with blood-red fire snaking down the middle and widening fast.

Brianna dropped to a crouch on the suddenly much thinner wall, clutching the strap of Nick's bag, which she had nearly dropped in her alarm. In her mind, she was the deer again—no, she was the deer and the human Brianna at the same time—instincts sharp, reflexes swift, an animal ready to flee for its life.

She was on the other half of the wall, the one that wasn't veering off into the darkness, but Nick had been caught with one set of paws on either side, and the gap had already widened too much for him to jump in either direction; in another moment he would fall down into the darkness between. Brianna flung the bag behind her and lunged to grab the wolf around the middle. He was much heavier than she had expected, and for a long, horrible moment she was sure they were both going down together.

She threw her weight backward, and they went over the other side of the wall. And didn't fall. She heard a tearing noise, and opened her eyes—embarrassed to find she had squeezed them shut—to see that they were hanging off a heavy curtain that Nick had caught in his claws and teeth. She let go of him with one hand to grab a handful of curtain herself, and let herself down until she was close enough to the floor to drop easily. Nick let go too, and twisted impressively in the air to land on his feet.

"Well!" said Brianna, smoothing her hands over her jeans to hide the fact that they were shaking. "That was fun!"

She looked around the room, which seemed to be a fancy living room, and was quite empty. Nick shook himself and trotted over to the bag that she had dropped. Brianna turned her back on him and sat on one of the couches. After a minute, human Nick came around from behind the couch, dressed in his T-shirt and pyjama pants, and dropped down beside her, pushing back his hair with a sigh.

"What was *that* about?"

He shook his head. "I don't know. Thanks for saving me."

"Oh, that's okay. That was Rose's daughter from the future?"

"Seems like it."

"Rose is human, right? So if her daughter is like that ... what's her husband?"

"Ex-husband. She's divorced, or separated or something. Anyway, I don't think he's the father of her kid. I don't know who is." He added this last bit hastily, in a way that made Brianna think he had an idea.

She didn't try to worm the answer out of him; she had a more general question that she had started to wonder about. "How many ... how many kinds of things are there? I mean, there's fairies, werewolves, vampires ... " She ticked them off on her fingers. "Yokai—what else?"

"I don't know, exactly. Most things, I think. All the Greek stuff—nymphs and satyrs and all that—and like gnomes and brownies and that kind of thing." He shrugged. "I don't know all the technical terms."

"What about you—how did you get turned into a werewolf?"

"Actually, I didn't. I was born a werewolf. It didn't sort of show up until I was thirteen, but it was always going to happen. I'm the seventh son of a seventh son."

"I thought that was supposed to be a lucky thing."

"Depends who you ask. My dad's Portuguese, and they have a tradition about it. He says his mom always told him, ever since he was a boy, to be careful not to have seven sons, because the youngest would end up being a werewolf—but he never took it seriously."

"Wow. So does he know?"

Nick nodded. "He's the only one. The first time it happened—the first time I turned into the wolf—my dad was the one who found me, and he kind of figured out what was up because of what my grandmother had always said about the seven sons. And we managed to keep it secret from everybody else. Sometimes I think maybe he's told my mom, but then it always turns out he hasn't."

"So … it's kind of like a genetic disease or something. I mean, you're not like the fairies, who are just a totally different species—you've got two human parents."

"Yeah, that's right. And I'm not like Cristina, who got turned into a vampire in New York in the eighties and bears the whole world a grudge about it."

"Oh, is that what her problem is?"

He grinned. "Yeah, that's part of it." He dragged himself up from the couch with another sigh. "We'd better get back to work looking for our peeps."

"Are you going to transform again?"

"Nah. It's kind of a hassle not being able to talk. And I can't always make it work a bunch of times in a row—it's like I need to recharge. I'll just have to grow a pair and deal with the weirdness up there myself."

She thought it was funny how he talked about himself and the wolf as if they were two different people.

"How do we get back up there?" Brianna asked, getting up from the couch and grabbing Nick's empty schoolbag. Now that they were down inside one of the rooms, the ceiling had appeared above them, looking perfectly solid. "Can we go out the door and get back to the kitchen?"

"Yeah, we probably could," said Nick. "But let me try something else first."

He pulled a chair over to the fireplace at one end of the room, and cleared a couple of candlesticks and vases off the deep marble mantel. He used the chair to climb up onto the mantel, from which he could easily reach the ceiling. He closed one hand into a fist and punched the ceiling.

"Ouch," he said shaking out his hand.

"Did you think it was just an illusion?" Brianna suggested, standing by the fireplace and looking anxiously up.

"Not exactly. But that worked when Tacky did it." He stood for a moment with his fingertips on the ceiling, looking at it thoughtfully. Then he tried again, and this time, because he was looking down when he drove his fist into the ceiling, Brianna saw his eyes flare shiny yellow-green for a moment. She started back. It was only when she heard Nick say, "Yes!" that she noticed he had succeeded in punching a hole in the ceiling.

He clambered down and grabbed the poker from beside the fireplace, and used it to enlarge the hole until he could haul himself up through. Chunks of plaster spattered down, which they hadn't done when he'd punched the hole in the first place. Brianna climbed onto the mantel after him, and was ready when he reached back through the hole to help pull her up. She didn't want to slow him down.

In the distance, she could see Tacky standing on the wall above the kitchen. He held out his hands in a puzzled gesture.

"What's going on?" he called across to them.

"Nothing!" Nick called back. "Everything's under control!"

Brianna wondered if that was a smart idea, but she said nothing.

They found Ms. Baker by herself in what looked like a dentist's waiting-room, flipping through an old *People* magazine. She had obviously adopted a version of Cristina's strategy of staying still and waiting for help. Nick was again impressed with her cool demeanour. She still looked half-tree, and she only started slightly when her daughter and Nick dropped down from the ceiling in front of her. They both began trying to explain the situation, and she nodded patiently.

"I see you never did find the bathroom," she said, looking at Brianna, who still had dried fairy-goo on her clothes and in her braids.

"*Mom*," Brianna groaned.

"It was just an observation, sweetheart."

Nick headed for the door of the dentist's office, which opened once again onto the bamboo corridor back to the 7C kitchen. Brianna and her mother followed him in.

They were halfway down the corridor, and Brianna was explaining to her mother how she'd got separated from Ms. Gianelli, when the ground beneath them began to shudder as though with an earthquake. The bamboo stalks on either side of the path trembled, and the green light that surrounded them started to fade. Nick quickened his pace.

"Is this normal?" he heard Denise ask behind him.

"Um … " said Brianna.

A wind began to tear through the tops of the bamboo, whipping the leaves together in a frenzy of green. Nick looked over his shoulder at Denise and Brianna.

"Should we run?" said Brianna.

"I think so," said Nick.

They ran, grabbing Denise by the hands to help her along. Rain had begun to pelt the bamboo grove by the time they reached the far end, and the earth was heaving violently. They tumbled out onto the dry, stable floor of the kitchen. Cristina was still sitting at the table, and Tacky was perched on the wall above the sink.

"What the fuck was that?" Nick demanded.

"I don't know," said Tacky. He stood up, looking away into the attic. "There is someone else up here." He glared back over his shoulder at Nick. "This will be somehow your fault, I know."

"My fault? No way—she's not *my* daughter!"

"I don't think you should have admitted that you know who it is," Brianna muttered as Tacky strode away along the wall.

"Good call," said Nick.

He wondered whether he had admitted to knowing more than that, and whether it would matter. Tacky might choose to ignore the hint that he had guessed who Jasmine's father was. It would be like Tacky to do that.

"Looking for me?" came a woman's voice from above the front door.

Nick spun around and looked up. Jasmine was grown up now, in her twenties. Her hair was cut short in a sleek style that fell over one eye, and she wore a slinky black-and-gold cheongsam and high-heeled shoes. She looked like a movie villain.

Tacky appeared on the opposite wall.

"Jasmine," he said.

He knew her name. Interesting.

"Takehiko," she purred. "So nice to *finally* meet you."

196

"*Nǐ juéduìguò bu lái,*" said Tacky.

Jasmine tossed back her curtain of sleek hair. "Speak English, will you? My Mandarin is *so* rusty—ever since my grandparents stopped talking to us."

Takehiko gave her a long, appraising look. *Mandarin?* Nick thought. *Grandparents?* What was *that* about?

"Who is this bitch?" Cristina demanded.

"*Yurusenai,*" Tacky said finally, drawing out the syllables. "You understand that one?"

"'I will not forgive you,'" Brianna translated in an undertone. "They say that all the time in anime."

"It's a challenge of some sort, isn't it?" said Jasmine carelessly. She'd let her hair fall back in her face, and now she held out one hand, curling fingers with claw-like black-painted nails, and little tongues of blood-red fire danced on their tips.

"You come from a future which I will not accept," said Takehiko.

"Oh, really? What's that supposed to mean?"

"It means I will send you back."

"I'd like to see you try!"

Tacky nodded. "You will."

He sprang across the open space above the kitchen. Jasmine flung a rope of red fire at him; it spooled out from her palm, an elegant, lethal-looking attack. He grabbed it in mid-air, coiling it around his wrist as if it were a real rope, and yanked on it, toppling her off the wall. She flailed for a moment, startled, but quickly caught herself and landed neatly by the sink, her high heels clicking on the counter. Tacky landed on the kitchen table.

"Oh ho!" said Jasmine, going for a sexy pose that didn't quite work. "You can fight, can you? I didn't know that about—" She broke off as a flower of blue *ki* began to blossom under her feet, gently lifting her off the counter. "What the—"

"What's he doing?" Brianna whispered to Nick.

"I'm—not sure."

"He's not setting her on fire?"

"No, nothing like that."

He remembered the way Tacky's *ki* had surrounded him that night in the midst of Stake's hunt. It looked like the blue cup shape rising up around Jasmine was doing the same thing. She batted angrily at it, but it continued to rise, following the shape that Takehiko was sketching in the air with his outstretched hands.

"Stop it! I won't go back!"

"You will," said Tacky.

"I *won't*!" She stamped her foot angrily, and Nick realized with a start that she was a little girl again, the age she had been in the gymnastics school.

She put her hands on the blue surface that had risen up around her waist, and screwed up her face with determination. Red sparks danced around the edge of the blue ring, and Nick could feel the tension in the air as she and Tacky fought it out.

Nick decided to try to intervene. "You have to go back, Jasmine. Come on—it's not fair to your mom. If you stay grown up, she'll have missed your whole childhood. *You* remember it, but she doesn't."

"I don't care about that," Jasmine said, scrunching her face in furious determination. But she wasn't making any progress against Tacky's growing blue orb. "I don't care about her."

Nick tried again. "But—maybe if you go back and start over, and do things over, you would. Don't you want that?"

"Why would I want that?"

"Because … uh … "

Brianna jumped in. "Because being friends with your mom is great. It's really great, it's one of the neat things about becoming a woman, getting to know your mom like a grown-up—and your dad, if you've got a dad—"

"I don't! And nothing's going to change that." She was losing the battle badly now. The blue orb was growing up around her shoulders.

"I don't either," said Brianna, "and it sucks, it does—but I've got an awesome mom, and so do you. I met her, you know, she helped me out. Nick can tell you, too—she's amazing. Right, Nick? I think you'd really like her if you gave her a chance."

"No way," Jasmine snarled. "I hate her. She's depressed all the time because my dad left her, and her friends got killed, and her bakery got blown up, and blah blah blah." She folded her arms sullenly as the veil of blue crept up over her face.

"Wait, what?" said Nick. "Her bakery got *blown up*?"

Jasmine sighed dramatically. "Not *blown up*." It sounded like she was speaking underwater now. "Like … went out of business or whatever. These people from … I don't know, Silver something, they did a big raid at Hallowe'en the year I was born, and killed her customers, and then she got shut down by the government. It's like the only thing she even cares about—she *doesn't* care about me."

"But she will, Jasmine," Brianna persisted. "You just have to give her another chance."

Nick was worrying about something else.

"Wait, wait." He ran around in front of the table to get Tacky's attention. "Should we try to get more details about what's going to happen at Hallowe'en before you send her back?"

Tacky glanced down at him. "I can't just keep her like this. She's the one who can ... change time—I have to—use her power against her, to—" He shook his head. Inside the blue bubble, the preteen Jasmine shrank into a toddler Jasmine with pigtails, still pouting. "I have to send her back."

"But is this one of these future things where if you go back and change one thing, it'll happen differently, or is it the kind of thing where you can't escape your destiny, or—I mean, should we be worried about this raid?" Nick was babbling now.

"I don't know," Tacky said irritably. "I don't know why you think I would."

He had a point.

The bubble of *ki* had closed over Jasmine's head now, and she shrank again, and this time went on shrinking, as the bubble tightened and thickened around her, until she was a tiny baby, floating curled up in a cloudy blue sphere about the size of her mother's womb.

"Ew," said Nick involuntarily, and caught Brianna giving him an disgusted look.

"Great," said Cristina. "She was prophesying, and you turn her into a baby. We're all going to die."

"Shut up," said Nick. "You don't know that."

"Guys?" said Brianna. "He's not finished, you know. He's still got to put her back into her mom."

It was true; Tacky leapt across the kitchen to where the blue orb hovered, and floated it up above the wall, where he disappeared with it into the darkness of the attic.

Nick climbed onto the counter by the sink, and by stepping on the windowsill, managed to reach up and grasp the top of the wall and pull himself clumsily up onto it. In the distance, he could see Tacky with the blue glow that contained the unborn Jasmine.

He looked out at the expanding web of rooms. He wanted to make himself useful, but he had no clue where to look for Ms. Gianelli. He thought about how he'd managed to punch a hole in the ceiling. It had been a bit like the trick he used to get on the Paths; he'd pulled a bit of his wolf self out from inside, but not let it come out all the way. He tried it again.

Yes, there it was: the scent of Orange Sneakers, snaking through the air like smoke. He almost laughed aloud. It was just like the way it worked in *The Legend of Zelda.*

When he let go of the wolf, like dropping a handful of water back into a pool, he lost the image of the scent threading through the darkness, but he remembered where it had come from. It was a room not far away in a particularly torturous chain that looped and doubled back on itself. He set off along the walls, picking his way carefully but with determination.

The room, when he reached it, proved to be his own bedroom, the room in his parents' house that he had shared with his brother Pedro. Ms. Gianelli was standing in the middle of it, arms folded, glaring up at the person lying on the top of the bunk-bed. And of course the person lying on the bed was Nick.

It was as weird, and almost as unpleasant, as when the person in the Sanderson Library had walked through him. He knew he was looking at a younger version of himself—he hadn't been back in that bedroom since he left home last fall, and he doubted Pete had kept the bunk-bed or the same posters on the walls. He looked younger, too; he must have been about Brianna's age. But it wasn't like looking at a picture, or even a video of himself. It was much creepier than that. He was very close to past-Nick, because the top of the bunk-bed came up uncomfortably close to the ceiling, meaning that you had to crawl in and out—the only reason Pete hadn't used his elder-brother privilege to claim the top for himself. He felt as if he could have reached out and touched his past self, though of course his hand would have gone right through him. The thought made him queasy.

"Young man," Ms. Gianelli was saying, for what was obviously the umpteenth time, "are you listening to me?"

Nick—present-day Nick, on top of the wall—groaned in disgust. Still in denial, then. Brianna had said she was, but he'd been hoping that after wandering through the impossible series of rooms produced by the panicked apartment for a while longer, Ms. Gianelli might have at least started to come to her senses. Since she hadn't, for him to drop down through the ceiling into a room that he was already technically in wasn't going to be particularly easy for her to take. He wondered whether he could convince her that the boy on the bed was his deaf twin brother.

Before he'd made up his mind about this, Nick-in-the-past swung himself sideways out of the top bunk and landed on the floor. Ms. Gianelli jumped back with an irritated exclamation. Nick-in-the-present realized what was going to happen next. He remembered that day. It had been a bad one. He'd meant to get out of the house first, but it had come over him suddenly.

Past-Nick dropped to his hands and knees on the floor in front of Ms. Gianelli, and changed into the wolf. It happened awkwardly, as it had in those early days; there was a moment when he gritted his teeth and looked like he was trying to resist it, which he was, and then slowly and painfully his human form dissolved into a smokey nothing, then coalesced again into the form of the wolf. He hadn't got his clothes off, so the wolf was tangled up in plaid shirt and jeans and had to thrash his way free, snapping and growling. It must have been the straw that broke the camel's back, seeing that. Ms. Gianelli drew a deep breath and screamed a full-throated, heartfelt scream. The wolf, of course, ignored her.

Nick swung down from the top of the wall to the bunk-bed, and dropped from there to the floor. Ms. Gianelli glanced between him and the wolf, and her scream died out in a puzzled whimper.

"It's okay," said Nick hastily. "Sorry to scare you."

"Wait," she said. "You're older. I thought you looked different—I mean he looked different. So this was all ... 'shadows of things that have been'?"

"Yeah, totally. That's a really good way of putting it."

"It's Dickens. So now, are you still a werewolf? Wait a minute—you were the wolf in the park, weren't you?"

"Yep."

"Yes, you said so at the time, I remember. Now why was I so slow to put the pieces together?"

"I think you were under a fairy spell?" Nick ventured.

Ms. Gianelli folded her arms again and gave him a severe look. "That doesn't sound very likely, now does it?"

"No-o ... but, um ... " He found her surprisingly intimidating now that she was in her right mind.

"But I just watched you turn into a wolf. In the past." She nodded, and then shuddered as the wolf walked casually through her leg.

"So if you'll just follow me," said Nick, heading for the door.

"What's that?" she asked, looking out at the bamboo corridor, which was dark and rainswept but no longer actively seismic.

"This? Uh, it's really hard to explain. But it'll take us back to where everybody else is."

"Hm," she said, but she followed him out into the corridor.

Denise and Brianna were sitting at the table with Cristina when they arrived in the kitchen.

"Hey Ms. G.," said Brianna, waving.

"Sandra," Denise greeted her. "You're all right?"

"I'm fine. What on earth has happened to you, Denise? Is that—" she looked at Nick. "Another fairy spell?"

"Pretty much. But she's gonna be okay."

"Good heavens."

"She will be fine," said Cristina, deadpan. "We will all die, though."

Nick glared at her. "I don't know what you're worried about. Aren't you technically already dead?"

"It does not mean I can't be killed again."

"Whatever. Is Tacky not back from … "

"No," said Brianna. "Look." She pointed at the kitchen ceiling.

It took Nick a moment to figure out what he was looking at. Oh. The kitchen ceiling.

"How long has that been there?"

"Just a couple of minutes. We were worried you wouldn't be able to get back through that bamboo place."

"No, it was okay this time. I don't know—maybe Tacky knows what he's doing."

"You could go up and see, couldn't you?" Brianna suggested. "I mean, you got through the ceiling in that other room."

"Yeah," said Nick sceptically. "I did, but … "

There was a knock at the front door. Everyone started, as if that were the weirdest thing that could possibly happen. Then Denise and Brianna looked at one another and laughed.

"That's just a real door, right?" said Brianna. "It's just somebody knocking at the real front door of your apartment."

"Yeah," said Nick, heading across the kitchen. People didn't normally knock at the front door of 7C, though. People couldn't normally find it.

The fairy second from the duel was standing on the porch, leaning casually on the railing, twitching his transparent insect wings in the sunlight. He reached out a lazy hand and made a flicking motion in Nick's direction, and Nick reeled backward, feeling as if someone had just kicked him hard in the stomach. He made an undignified landing amid the potted plants around the entrance. The fairy strode into the kitchen.

"We've become aware of a problem," he said in his fruity voice. He smiled toothily at Ms. Gianelli. "Hello there."

"You!" Ms. Gianelli cried, not so much frightened as outraged. She glanced between Denise and the fairy. "I—you—I remember what you did!"

"Yes," said the fairy languidly. "That's the problem. I left you with a nice dose of denial to make things easy for you, but you seem to have shaken it off, and it's *all terribly inconvenient*. I'll have to ask you to come with me."

"I'm not going anywhere with you!" Ms. Gianelli retorted. "You're an evil fairy!"

Brianna had crept around behind the fairy to where Nick was picking himself up from the floor.

"Honestly," she whispered, "I think I liked her better when she was in denial."

"You tried to turn my colleague into a *tree*!" Ms. Gianelli went on. "You can't just do that kind of thing—she's a respected staff member! Who's going to take the girls' volleyball team to the finals next week? They were favoured to win in our division!"

"I don't know, actually," Nick whispered back. "There's a weird degree of awesomeness about this."

The fairy heaved a huge sigh. "I *hate* having to do this," he remarked to the room as a whole. "It's so overused— such a cliché." He twitched his wings and waved a hand at Ms. Gianelli, and with a startled yelp, she began to melt.

Nick noted that the process was quite different from what it had looked like when he turned into the wolf in his childhood bedroom. She remained opaque and more or less solid the whole time, just changing shape and colour, shifting and dripping and compacting down from human form to something small and slimy.

"A toad?" said Cristina scornfully. "That *is* cliché."

"No!" Denise cried.

Brianna dove past the fairy and scooped the toad up off the floor.

"Oh, now really," said the fairy irritably. He waved his hand again, and the toad began to drip between Brianna's fingers.

Nick reached Brianna's side in time to catch the slippery wet fish that flopped toward the kitchen floor. Denise pushed back her chair and got to her feet. The fish squirted out of Nick's grasp, and Denise staggered forward to scoop it up. In another moment she was struggling with an armload of something clawed and furry. Brianna lunged in and grasped a striped tail, and the next moment Nick, plunging into the fray again, found himself in sole possession of a huge snake.

"I got this one," he gasped, as the snake wound its way crushingly around his arm. "Cristina—plug in the modem by the toaster, will you?"

"The what?"

"The modem—that thing with—"

"I've got it," said Brianna, running around the table toward the counter.

"Plug it in—over by the toaster—on the … " Nick grabbed the snake's head and tried to wrench it away from his throat.

"I haven't the faintest idea what that would do," said the fairy languidly, "but I obviously can't allow it."

He waved a hand at Brianna.

For a moment it looked as though she was running through molasses. Then it looked as though she was turning into molasses herself. She was slowly losing her form, but she kept moving toward the counter and the modem, resisting his magic.

"Oh, that thing!" said Cristina, seeing what Brianna was going for.

She made a move toward the counter herself. The blind covering the window by the fridge snapped up, and sunlight flashed into the room. Cristina flung herself backward with a howl, crashing into the table and knocking over a chair.

Something silver flew across the room and clunked on the fairy's forehead. He staggered slightly, more confused than anything. He glared across the table at Denise.

"Did you just throw a spoon at me?"

"It was the nearest thing to hand," she said. "But give me another moment. The knife block is right over there."

The fairy looked around sharply for the knife block, but Denise had been bluffing—there wasn't one. Brianna was looking more cat that human now, but she had managed to plug in the modem. Nick had been too busy keeping the snake from wrapping itself around his throat to see how she had done it. The lights on the front began to flash as it initialized itself.

Cristina surged out from under the table, lunging for the fairy. Her hair was smoking and frizzled, and her fangs gleamed.

"Ugh," said the fairy, sidestepping fastidiously. "Who *are* you people?"

He flapped a hand at the snake, and it began to unwind itself from Nick's arm and balloon outward into something heavy and hairy. A hoof slammed into Nick's stomach, and he rolled away, gasping. When he could take stock of his surroundings again, Brianna and her mother between them were struggling to hold onto a plunging and bucking horse that had already trampled one of the kitchen chairs. Brianna's form seemed to have stabilized: she had whiskers and black cat ears poking up between her braids, but otherwise she was still basically human. The fairy was standing in the middle of the square of sunlight from the window, keeping a wary distance from Cristina, who was hissing at him from the edge of the shade. The lights on the modem had stopped blinking and shone steady green.

Nick gathered himself up and scooted out of the way of the horse's stamping hooves. The hall door opened to admit Takehiko and Rose. The fairy slewed around to stare at them. Takehiko glared back, yellow-eyed.

"You guys took your time," said Nick.

Tacky flashed his yellow-eyed glare at Nick. He threw something down on the floor by the washing machine. Nick was startled to see it was one of his favourite combat boots.

It was Rose who spoke first, after taking in the whole scene and looking back at the fairy standing in the sun under the window.

"What do you think you're doing?" she asked sternly.

"Just a bit of necessary damage control," he said with a false casualness.

"Not in my house, you're not."

"No? Well, I quite see that. You must enforce your sovereignty over your own people, and all that."

"Please be so good as to return them to their human forms before you leave."

"Oh, those two? Well, yes. I do see how you might prefer that." He waved a hand. "There you go."

Ms. Gianelli crumpled to the floor in her orange jacket, ropes of green goo decorating her smart glasses and dripping from her hair. Denise, who had been clinging to the horse's back, landed on top of her, and Brianna helped her to her feet. Brianna's cat-nose and ears were gone as well.

"That will do," said Rose. "Thank you. Cristina, will you please let him leave?"

Cristina gave an irritable snarl, but stepped aside.

"Humans for the win," said Nick.

Tacky stalked across the kitchen after the fairy, making sure he went straight to the door. When he reached it, the fairy turned back and looked Tacky in the eye.

"You don't know what she gave up for your sake," he remarked. "But we do."

Takehiko held the door open for him and said nothing.

That evening, Brianna sat at the kitchen table with Nick and Takehiko. They were drinking tea and eating pecan pie straight out of the pie plate with forks. Ms. Gianelli had gone home, and Cristina and Rose had long since gone back down to the bakery. Brianna's mother was asleep on the couch in the living room, and a bed had been made up for Brianna in one of the spare bedrooms. She'd had a long bath and was free of green fairy gunk, and though she slightly missed her cat ears and whiskers—she'd liked that transformation much better than the deer—she was glad to finally feel like herself again. She'd had a tour of the real 7C, and heard about how the rooms worked, when they weren't malfunctioning, and about the little satyr who used to live here.

"For the four millionth time," Nick said, "I didn't drop the boot on purpose, okay? I was falling into a fucking black chasm of—"

"Yes," said Takehiko. "I know about that. Where do you think I had to go down to get it out?"

"I didn't do it on purpose," Nick persisted, "and I didn't know it was going to gum up the works or whatever and keep the apartment from changing back to normal. Obviously I had no idea you'd have to go down … " He shuddered and couldn't finish the sentence. "And I'm *sorry*, okay?"

Takehiko shrugged. "Whatever."

Brianna thought about the frightening black fissures between the multiplying rooms. Just looking down from the top of the walls had been bad enough. And Tacky had gone down *into* one of them?

"How much of this did you tell Rose?" Nick asked.

Takehiko had taken a big bite of pie, and used the excuse of having his mouth full not to say anything for a minute. "Placticary—practically—nothing," he admitted finally.

"Yeah," said Nick. "That's what I figured." He sighed. "I'm not volunteering to do it myself, by the way. But she probably does need to be told. I mean, it was Jasmine who was making the rooms move through time, wasn't it?"

Tacky nodded. "I think yes."

"So she's pretty powerful, right?" said Brianna.

"Mm."

"Kind of makes you wonder who her father is, huh?" said Nick.

"Does it?" said Tacky, stabbing his fork into the pie again and coming away with another large hunk.

"Yeah, but more importantly, what she said about the bakery being attacked, was that something that's going to actually happen, or … "

"But she was kind of like a figment, wasn't she?" said Brianna. "I mean, all of the time-travel things were figments— you could walk through the people and everything. So maybe she was Rose's daughter from an imaginary future that won't really happen."

"That's what I'm hoping," said Nick. "Anyway, we probably don't have to worry about telling Rose anything—Cristina'll probably take care of that. Prophecies of doom aren't the kind of thing Cristina can keep to herself."

They ate pie in silence for a bit.

"Why was it so important to plug the modem back in?" Brianna asked.

"I didn't know that it necessarily was," Nick admitted. "I just thought it was worth a try."

"Hm," said Tacky. "That was what happened."

"What?"

He waved his fork vaguely. "I can't explain, but … it made it easier to find your stupid boot."

"Well, that was Brianna. She plugged the modem back in—I was too busy wrestling a snake. And she was half a cat when she did it, too. It was pretty amazing."

Tacky gave Brianna a respectful nod.

She leaned back in her chair, buzzed with tea and sugar, and tired from a very long, very weird day. Nick and Tacky went on talking, bickering about exactly what the computer network did and how that might or might not have interfered with Jasmine's time-manipulating powers and the multiplying rooms. Brianna wondered if Cristina was even now, down in the bakery, explaining to Rose that her unborn daughter had been wandering around dressed like a video-game avatar, picking fights with her tenants and prophesying doom. And what about what the fairy had said at the end—*you don't know what she gave up for your sake*—what did that mean?

Brianna's mom was going to have to stay at 7C until her tree parts returned to normal, which would take at least a week. Brianna was looking forward to it. Nick had already offered to drive her to school, though it was really not too far to walk. He was such a nice guy, she thought. She watching him arguing with Takehiko, and thought again about what a cute couple they would make.

"And so ... *who* set up the network, again?" Nick asked.

Takehiko gave him a disgusted look. "I said. A guy. I can't. Talk about."

"Wait, you still can't talk about him?"

"Will you shut up? If I keep talking about how I can't talk about him, soon I won't be able to think about him even." He sipped his tea, and added after a moment, "It probably does not matter. I think that he is dead."

"I've gotta say," said Nick, leaning back in his chair, "I'm really done with having epic battles in this kitchen. Though at least this one didn't leave us with as much clean-up as that pigeon business."

"Pigeon business?" Brianna repeated.

"Oh yeah," said Nick. "It was wild. We'll tell you about it some time."

BONUS PAGES

THE FUTURE

October 2013

TO NICK, WHO HAD been used to a household filled with older brothers, it was strange to live in an apartment with only one other person. It was weirdly quiet. Then there was his roommate. Rose had explained that Takehiko had come out of a four-hundred-year-old painting, and wasn't entirely used to life in this century. Nick had thus been vaguely prepared for someone who said "thee" and "thou" and thought that the television was witchcraft. Takehiko was not like that at all. He dressed like a fashion magazine, and had got further in *Final Fantasy XIV* than Nick. Every so often, though, he would come out with some weird question. For instance:

"Have you ever been to Mars?"

"Where?" Nick's first thought was that he was talking about some downtown club; it seemed like the sort of thing he might ask about.

"Mars," Takehiko repeated. "The Mars Coro … Colony. Have you been there?"

"No. I don't even know what you're talking about."

"Is it not well known? I saw a television show where people are talking about it. They said there is a … revo-ryu-tion in the Mars Corony, I think, and I wonder if you have been there, and what happened."

"Okay … I think you were watching a science fiction show."

"What does that mean?"

"It means it's made up."

"I know *that*. I am not stupid. I know that the people are actors."

"Yeah, and the story's not real, either."

"There was no revo-yution on Mars?"

"There's no *colony* on Mars. There's no aliens, there's no hyperspace drive, there's no Intergalactic whatever-the-fuck. It's science fiction."

"Are you sure there is none of these, or is it like were-wolves, maybe, that other people think there are not, but really there are?"

"No. I'm sure. I mean—yes, there could be aliens, maybe, but nobody knows about that, and what you saw was definitely science fiction. It sounds like it was probably *Babylon 5*."

"Yes! That is the name of the place, the … "

"The space station. The *made-up* space station."

"Oh."

"The idea is … it's supposed to be in the future."

"Oh, I see. Because of time travel."

"Wh … No. There's no time travel either."

"Then how do they show all of those things?"

"It's not real. It's all computer graphics and stuff."

"Mm." He appeared to think about this for a while. Then he said: "But there are really people who are all fake like puppets, with their brains inside. Yes?"

"What? With their … Um … Cyborgs?"

"Yes."

"No."

"No?"

"No. I think you need to stop watching the Space channel."

"I am trying to learn about the world."

"Well, watch the news or something."

"What if I can't tell the difference? Why do they have these made up shows about the future? It is very confusing."

"It's not supposed to be educational programming for idiots out of the seventeenth century."

"I am not an idiot. I understand about this now. Also, I saw a show with giant lizards—I think this is science fishing as well, *ne*? Giant dragon lizards—but not smart like real dragons, just stupid like animals."

"You don't mean dinosaurs, do you?"

"Yes. I do."

"Well, they're not science fiction—didn't you *listen* to the show? Dinosaurs are real. I mean—"

"Where are they?"

"Nowhere now—they lived way in the past."

"No—*I* lived in the past, and I have never seen them."

"*Way* in the past. Millions of years before you were born."

"Millions of years. But there is no time travel."

"No, people dug up their bones and stuff."

"Oh! Yes, they said this in the show. I see. I did not know why they were always talking about bones. So. Science fishing is in the future, dinosaurs are the past. You can't tell when I am joking, can you?"

"What? How much of that was joking?"

"None of it. I was just saying."

"What?"

"If I had been joking, I think you could not tell."

"But … if you *weren't*, you don't know that. And … you weren't, right?"

"You see? *You* don't know."

"You are a colossal asshole. Just … colossal."

But there was something oddly comforting about that, Nick thought. Takehiko might be only one person instead of six, but he was clearly going to make up for it by being more of an incomprehensible jerk than any of Nick's brothers. So that was all right. His world made sense again.

THE PRESENT

(A 7C CHRISTMAS STORY)

December 2013

"WHAT IS IT?" NICK called irritably, pushing himself up onto his elbows in bed.

The door opened a little, and Takehiko leaned in on an angle, his hair swinging past his shoulder to hang like a curtain.

"I just think I should tell you. There is a tree in the living room."

Nick blinked up at him. "Wha ... who ... what kind of a tree?"

"A sort of evergreen tree, with ... " He sketched circles in the air with the hand that was not holding onto the door. "With things all over it, hanging off of it."

"Oh. A Christmas tree." Nick lay back down. "I thought you meant there was a tree growing out of the floor or something."

"No, it is not growing. It is in some water, but it is not going to last very long like that."

"Yeah, well, Christmas is in a week."

"Why is it there?" Tacky persisted.

"I don't know—I guess the house put it there. I guess it knows Christmas is coming up."

"Mm. Is it a … lerligious thing?"

"Christmas? Yeah, it's—"

"No, the tree. I know Christmas, I am not stupid—but why does it have a tree?"

"I don't know." Nick yawned hugely. "It's just something you do. It's a tradition."

"Is it a sacred tree?"

"No, it's just a tree. You put decorations on it, and you put presents under it, and—"

"What, you give it presents, but it is not a sacred tree?"

"No! The presents aren't *for* the tree, numbskull. They're for your family and stuff."

"But you offer them to the tree … "

"No, you don't." He looked at Takehiko for a moment. "You're having me on again, aren't you? This is like the time you pretended to think *Battlestar Galactica* was a documentary, isn't it?"

Tacky ignored this. "Do you think I should put a present under the tree, in case it gets angry? It will soon be dead, but if it is a sacred tree … "

"Yeah, you should," said Nick, rolling over to face the wall. "You should buy me an iPhone. And put it under the tree. I think that should definitely appease it." He pulled the covers over his head and went back to sleep.

He got up later that morning, to answer a phone call. It was his father, and the conversation ended with Nick shouting that if it was going to be like that, he wasn't coming home for Christmas at all. When he finally went into the living room, he had forgotten all about the tree. The living room was all in white and unfinished wood that week, with wicker baskets, the bookshelves concealed behind frosted glass. The Christmas tree stood in one corner, tastefully decorated with iridescent glass balls and small white lights. Something lay on the floor under its lowest boughs: something white and silver, with a bundle of white wires. Nick bent down and stared. It was an iPhone. Sitting on top of it was a little stylized wolf folded out of silver wrapping paper.

Takehiko was in the kitchen, watering the plants on the window-ledge near the fridge.

"Where did this come from?" Nick demanded, brandishing the iPhone.

"I got it off the Internet. It's for you."

"These things are expensive—they're like hundreds of dollars. How did you ... you don't even have any money, do you?"

"Not really."

But that wasn't even the most perplexing thing. "That was just like a couple hours ago that I told you to get me one—and it was a *joke*, anyway—when did you buy this?"

"I told you, I didn't buy it—I got it off the Internet."

"You don't *get* things off the Internet, Tacky. You still have to pay for them."

"No, I don't." He was giving Nick the same look as when he had to explain to him how to use the rice cooker: the I'm-not-even-from-this-century-how-can-you-be-so-dumb? look. He set down the watering can. "I will show you."

Nick followed Tacky down the hall to his bedroom. In those days Nick had never been inside Tacky's bedroom, just looked into it from the doorway when he was trying to find his own room and failing.

"Lucky," he remarked, when the first door Tacky opened was the right one. Tacky gave him a look, and he remembered that it wasn't luck. The room, he noted, was disgustingly neat.

Tacky folded himself down onto the cushion in front of his low, coffee-table desk, as tidy as the origami wolf. He tapped at the keyboard of his computer to wake it. Even from the doorway, Nick had noticed Takehiko's computer. It was not, in his opinion, the sort of set-up that someone from the sixteenth century ought to have owned. A screen-saver of a Chinese dragon undulated across the giant display, and cables snaked over the desk to printer, scanner, speakers, all neatly arranged. The computer awoke with a purring of fans, and transparent windows full of Japanese text cascaded over a water-colour landscape.

"Is that ... Linux or something?" Nick asked, as Tacky closed windows and clicked through menus.

"Who?"

"The ... never mind. Where did you get this computer, anyway?"

"So it is very easy," said Tacky, ignoring the question.

He had opened a browser window; a banner at the top of the home page read *Bakemono.net* in elegant brushstrokes above columns of Japanese text and cartoony graphics. He tapped in a url, typing with two fingers but surprisingly fast.

"Amazon Japan?" Nick observed sceptically. "I'm pretty sure you have to pay for things there."

"It has to be somewhere with pictures. That is how it works." Tacky twirled the cursor around one of the images. "Pretend I want to get this thing."

"That's an electric razor. Do you even shave?"

Tacky ignored him. "Watch—I do this ... "

He speared the image of the razor with the cursor and

dragged it down to a round, glistening white icon at the bottom of the screen. The white icon bounced up and down a couple of times, and then was still. A dialogue box with a line of characters materialized.

"What does it say?"

"Pearl has accepted your request—items will be ... um, multiplified ... multiplicated?"

"Multiplied. *Multiplied*?"

"Multiplicated according to time. Or something. It is Chinese."

"Chinese?"

"I think many computer things come from China."

"That's ... true, but ... "

Tacky had reached over to twitch back a blue-and-white quilt that had been covering a bulky object on a shelf next to his desk. Nick stared in perplexity at what looked to him like a construction of Mechanos inside a fish-tank. Tacky flicked a switch at the side of this object, and a sort of syringe suspended from a rail at the top slid back and forth experimentally, with a soft whirring noise.

"What is that?" Nick demanded.

Takehiko shrugged. "It's a computer thing."

Nick peered at it. "Is it a 3D printer? It looks kind of like it might be a homemade 3D printer."

The hanging syringe began to fill, inexplicably, with a rose-coloured, uncomputerlike light. Then, in a series of movements too fast to follow precisely, it whizzed back and forth on its rail, while the rail moved on its own trajectory within the fish-tank, and the red light sketched out a complex three-dimensional object in the air. The light blinked out, there was a little *plunk*, and the electric razor from the computer screen lay on the black platform at the bottom of the fish-tank, sealed into its plastic package. Tacky reached in and extracted it. He handed it to Nick. The plastic was slightly warm to the touch.

"I see," said Nick. "That's how you got the iPhone." He set the packaged razor down on the desk. It was freaking him out a bit.

"Mm."

"That's ... Did the computer make the origami wolf as well?"

Takehiko looked at him incredulously. "Of *course not*. It is a computer."

"No, Tacky—it's a friggin' science fiction machine. Computers don't just *make things* like that. Even 3D printers—I've seen them work before, and they don't just produce random things from the Internet."

"They can make erect– um—elect ronic things only. That is their magic."

"Oh, for—the computer's not magic."

Tacky gave him a long look. "Yes, it is."

"Well ... yeah. That computer might be magic. But, like ... *computers* aren't magic."

Tacky shrugged. "Maybe the cheap ones that are not so good ... "

"No! I'm telling you, they don't normally do that—computers do not normally do that."

"Okay. So. People do not normally turn into wolves."

"Right." He lived in an apartment where the rooms moved around and the living room redecorated itself at will; he really shouldn't be surprised by these things any more. All the same, Nick looked doubtfully from the Mechano-filled fish-tank with its now empty syringe to the iPhone which it had apparently produced from thin air. "Are you sure it's okay for me to keep this thing? It isn't, like, the proceeds of crime, or ... necromancy or something?"

"It's a *Christmas present*," Takehiko retorted. He added, primly: "I understand Christmas presents."

"Do you? Because … you didn't seem to, before."

"No. I understand. You are not supposed to ask how much did it cost, are you sure you did not steal it off the Internet. You are just supposed to say thank you. 'It is the thought that counts.'"

"Yeah … I don't know what the thought was, exactly. But thanks. I mean, it is an awesome present." He turned towards the door, then stopped, and looked back at Tacky. "So if the computer didn't make the paper wolf, I guess you did."

"Mm."

"It's … cute."

Takehiko raised his eyebrows. "I did not try to be *cute*. I had to make sure the tree knew that the present was for you."

About the Author

Alice Degan is an academic and novelist (who also sometimes writes short stories). She studies and teaches medieval literature and writes fantasy and something she likes to call metaphysical romance. She lives in Toronto, in a weird house in an alley, where the rooms do in fact stay where you left them.

Join the Friends of 7C and keep up to date with the series:
www.alicedegan.com/7C

CPSIA information can be obtained at www.ICGtesting.com
Printed in the USA
LVOW10s1235190815

450722LV00001B/1/P